# ALEX SPARROW
## and the Furry Fury

More than anything else, this story is about kindness. So I dedicate it to Toby Cox – one of the kindest people I have ever known.

# ALEX SPARROW
## and the Furry Fury

by Jennifer Killick

Firefly

First published in 2018
by Firefly Press
25 Gabalfa Road, Llandaff North, Cardiff, CF14 2JJ
www.fireflypress.co.uk

A CIP catalogue record of this book is available from
the British Library.

print ISBN: 978-1-910080-74-0
ebook ISBN: 978-1-910080-75-7

This book has been published with the support of the
Welsh Books Council.

Typeset by Elaine Sharples
Original cover art by Heath McKenzie
Cover design by Alex Dimond

Printed and bound by Pulsio Sarl

# 1

## My Life as a Hero

'Agent A is back on da case; hunting 'dem pigs who off on da chase; picking up clues like he picks up da ladies; smellin' so fresh like a field of daisies…'

'Smelling like poo, you mean,' Jess snorted. 'You just stepped in some.'

'Oh, nuts,' I said, trying to scrape it off my school shoe. 'Mum's going to kill me.'

'Anyway, ladies doesn't rhyme with daisies.'

'It would be easier to freestyle if you laid me

down some sick beats, Jessticles,' I said. 'But of course you're in too much of a mood.'

'I never thought I'd say this, but I wish you'd go back to the narration thing. It was slightly less annoying.' Jess bent down to look under a stack of PE equipment at the side of the games area.

'This is the first mission we've had in weeks.' I dropped into a crouch and sniffed at the ground like proper trackers do on TV. 'You could be a bit more enthusiastic.'

'Looking for Boris and Noodle is hardly a mission, Alex.'

'There are two ferocious beasts on the loose in the school grounds. We've been charged with protecting the innocent and bringing those thugs to justice.'

'They're guinea pigs.' Jess rolled her eyes so hard that I thought they might disappear into her brain cavity.

'That's right. And we're taking them in – dead or alive.'

I rubbed a bit of dirt between my fingers.

'You know that's poo too, right?'

'How's that poo?' I wiped my fingers on the ground. 'They look like little brown candies.'

Jess just sighed and looked at the sprinkles of poo leading out of the playground. She turned towards the school field. 'This way.'

'At least we know we're on their tails,' I said. 'Followin' da trail of candy-poo devastation; Agent A and moody J spy out their destination; A's majestic stealth don't need no explanation…'

'…But Alex's attempts at rapping are a sad abomination.'

'Now you're getting into the spirit of it, Jessticles,' I said, patting her on the shoulder with my poo fingers.

'Also, guinea pigs don't have proper tails.'

We made our way across the field towards the furthest corner, where the garden lived. It was November, and times were tough. As you probably know, I'm a pretty upbeat person, and I've always been like a flipping ray of sunshine compared to Jess. I was used to that. But in the aftermath of PALS and Miss Smilie, it was like she wanted life to go back the way it was before we got our powers. And I couldn't understand it. I tried not to let her bring me down, but it was getting harder. I'd thought that volunteering to look for Boris and Noodle would make her remember the good times, but it just seemed to pee her off even more.

'I think I can see something moving,' I said. 'Under that green leaf thing.'

'You mean the lettuce?' She looked at me like I was the most stupid person in the world.

'I'm not a vegetarian like you – I can't be expected to remember the names of *all* the vegetables.'

'The other day you said you didn't want to eat the orange stick thingy.'

'Well, I didn't. It tasted weird.'

'It was a carrot, Alex. A *carrot.*'

'What's your point, Jessticles?'

'My point is that it's the most basic of all the vegetables. Two year olds know what a carrot is.'

'My mind is way too busy with important business to worry about things like that.'

'You mean like your investigation of Miss Hussein?'

When Miss Smilie was arrested earlier in October, the school got a new teacher to replace her. She was called Miss Hussein and I was certain she was another bad guy in disguise, possibly planted by Montgomery McMonaghan and his corrupt organisation, SPARC. So I did what any good agent would do: I devoted my life to uncovering Miss Hussein's secret identity. I followed her. I asked her constant questions. I tried my hardest to make her mad and trick her into telling a lie. But the thing with Miss Hussein was that she was really, *really* nice. Like, so super-nice it was annoying.

We moved towards the vegetable patch: me with the stealth of a panther, and Jess with the clomp clomp of a buffalo. The sky had suddenly turned dark and it had started to rain freezing fat blobs of water. It was the perfect weather for our manhunt. I made a series of hand gestures and head movements to communicate to Jess what our plan should be without giving away our position.

'What?' she said.

It was quite dark so she must not have seen clearly. I did them again.

'Alex, it's cold and wet and I have no idea what you're trying to do.'

'I'm saying we should flank them, of course! Also – you ruin everything.'

'Whatever,' Jess said, and moved to the right of

the garden. At least she knew what flanking meant, that was something.

I took the left flank, sneaking like a shadow through the gloom towards my prey. The vegetable patch was like an unlidded box made of logs, about the size of a wrestling ring. It was filled with mud and leaves and freakish-looking scarecrows that the Reception kids made out of old Coke bottles.

And there was definitely something in amongst the vegetables. I braced myself for the pounce, for the beast to fight back. Instead, a white floppy-haired head poked out from under a leaf and squeaked. I looked over at Jess. Her special power isn't as useful as mine, obviously. But in this situation being able to talk to animals would come in handy. I used to laugh when I saw the twitch that came as the side effect of her power and happened whenever she talked to them, but even her twitching just wasn't the same anymore. She'd decided to have 'office hours' for her power, when animals were allowed to come see her with their requests. At other times, she didn't like talking to them – she said it got too tiring, what with all the Year 6 exam work we were doing at school. Now she twitched in the most bored way possible.

'Boris is surrendering,' Jess said. 'He doesn't like the rain and he wants to go back to his hutch.'

'Oh,' I said, feeling quite disappointed. 'Well, one down, one still on the loose.'

A golden-brown head peeped out next to Boris and managed to squeak through the mouthful of green leaf it was munching on.

Jess twitched and sighed. 'Noodle's surrendering too. He does whatever Boris does.'

'I think they were intimidated by my powerful presence,' I said.

'Let's just get them back to school before we're completely soaked.'

'Shouldn't we interrogate them about why they escaped?' I said, really hoping for a bit more excitement out of the situation.

'Alex,' Jess turned to me, 'they're guinea pigs. They got out of their hutch and stole some lettuce. Even you can't make this into a drama. Now grab Boris, and I'll get Noodle.'

'You grab Boris. He looks like he might bite.'

'Fine,' Jess huffed and scooped up Boris with an air of professionalism I had to respect.

I crept towards Noodle.

'There's no point tiptoeing, Alex. He's looking right at you. He already knows you're coming.'

'Right,' I said. 'Do guinea pigs have claws?'

'Would you like me to carry it back to the hutch?' An unfamiliar voice made me jump out of my skin, and Jess too from the look of it.

The new boy, Rex, had somehow walked across the entire field without us noticing, and was standing right behind us. He was almost as stealthy as me.

Jess frowned at him, not in an especially nasty way, just in the way she frowned at everyone except Dave. Rex had only been at Cherry Tree Lane for a week, and he'd been getting a hard time from the other kids. His uniform was old, even though he was new. His trousers were too short, his jumper was too big and his shoes looked like they'd come out of a dustbin. Also, he hardly talked, just stared the whole time like he was judging everyone. I hadn't picked on him, but I hadn't made an effort with him either. He was a bit weird.

'I'm used to dealing with animals,' Rex said. 'Me and my mum have just taken over the Cherry Tree Lane Animal Sanctuary.'

Jess's face lit up. Honestly, I'd been trying to cheer her up for weeks with very little success, and this guy rolls in with the words 'animal sanctuary' and she's practically smiling at him.

'Some help would be great,' Jess said. 'Alex is obviously afraid of the guinea pig.'

'I'm not afraid,' I said, my tiny white lie setting off my lie-detecting ear, which rumbled loudly and sent the odour of fart cutting through the damp naturey smell of the garden. 'He does have the eyes of a killer, though.'

Rex bent over the vegetable patch and laid his hands on the soil, palms facing up, and Noodle scampered out of the lettuce immediately. He sniffed at Rex's dirty fingernails and then hopped into his hands like he was his best mate or something.

'That's amazing,' Jess gasped in an infuriating way.

Rex just nodded like it was nothing and let Noodle cuddle into his jumper.

This was all it took for Jess to decide that the new boy was alright. I still had my doubts.

'Can I work at the animal sanctuary?' Jess asked. 'I could come in after school and on weekends. I'm good with animals, aren't I, Alex?' She turned to me, which was nice because I was wondering if she'd forgotten that I existed.

'Yeah, she's got a special way with animals,' I said.

Rex looked at me and then at Jess. 'We do need help. But we can't pay you.'

'Stuff that then,' I said. 'No pay, no way – that's what I always say.'

'You've literally never said that, Alex,' Jess glared at me. 'And I'll work for free; I just want the experience.'

'Wait, what?' I said. The girl was nuts.

'Ok, I'll ask my mum if we can give you a trial,' Rex nodded. 'I like the way you handle a guinea pig.'

He turned and started walking back across the field to the school, leaving Jess with a huge smile on her face.

'I like the way you handle a guinea pig,' I said, pulling my hat low on my forehead to try to keep the rain out of my eyes. 'Dat boy got game, son.'

# 2

## It Begins With an 'M' and Ends in an 'N'

'How can it not wake you up? It's the most horrific noise I've ever heard.' Jess yawned and picked at a scab on her elbow.

If anyone else had said that, I'd have expected my ear to fart extra juicily, but Jess was the biggest non-exaggerator in the world.

'And it's so loud,' Dave said. 'Maybe all that ear farting has damaged your hearing.'

It was lunchtime and we were sitting on what

used to be called the Friendship Bench, but was now called the Reflection Bench due to the whole school trying to avoid anything that sounded like it was in any way connected to PALS. PALS was the 'Positive Aspirational Life Skills' programme that our school decided to inflict upon us at the start of the year, but it didn't turn out so well. And after Miss Smilie was exposed by the amazing Agent Alex (that's me), they realised PALS actually stood for 'Pupil Automated Lobotomy Scheme'. People were pretty unhappy about it, and now the school was trying to act like it never happened. Anyway, they could call the bench whatever they liked – everybody still avoided sitting on it and being seen as a loser, which is why it was perfect for us. Wait – that came out wrong. I mean it was private and we could chat without anyone listening in. That's why it was perfect for us. We are most definitely not losers.

Anyway, Jess and Dave and everybody else in town were being kept awake at night by foxes. Loads of people were talking about it – it had even been on the news. Personally, I didn't see what all the fuss was about.

'It can't be that bad,' I said. 'They're just foxes, a.k.a. orange dogs.'

'It sounds like demons screaming from hell,' Jess said.

'I wonder if they've eaten Colin from next door. He's been missing for weeks.'

'Your next-door neighbour has gone missing?' Dave said. 'His poor family.'

'Meh, he was a scabby old thing anyway,' I said. 'I used to chase him out of my garden all the time.'

Dave looked confused.

'Colin is a cat, Dave,' Jess said.

'Maybe the foxes are performing some kind of dark ritual.' I imagined them dancing around a fire with Colin tied to a tree. 'That would explain these "alleged" (I did the annoying finger-quote thing) noises.'

'I can't believe anyone can sleep through them,' said Jess.

'What can I say? I'm especially skilled at sleeping.'

'Sleeping isn't a skill,' she huffed.

'You only say that because you're not good at it.'

'I'm too tired to even argue with you,' Jess said, yawning again and slumping back on the bench.

'And I bow down to your mastery,' Dave laughed. 'Teach me, oh wise one, for I am in desperate need of zees.'

'Don't encourage him, Dave.' Jess nudged him in the ribs but he didn't seem to mind.

'Well, before I go to bed, I like to have a largish snack,' I said. 'Because waking up from hunger is the worst. Something with cheese and ham, and then something with chocolate, or maybe…'

'What's going on over there?' Jess jumped up, rudely interrupting me, and ran over to where a crowd of kids had gathered by the climbing frame.

Me and Dave followed Jess, who was pushing her way through the mob. You'd think that after we saved them all from becoming blueberry muffins, brainwashed by Miss Smilie and PALS last half term, they'd show a bit of respect and stand aside for us, but life moves fast in the Juniors and last month's events had been pretty much forgotten. To be fair, Jess didn't need them to stand aside: when she was on the path to justice, nobody got in her way, not even Big Bad Bhavi.

As I fought my way through, I wasn't surprised

to hear Jason's voice shouting above all the rest. He used to be my best friend, but then I realised he was a total jerk. Apart from the odd comment under his breath, he'd pretty much stopped picking on me – I think because he was scared that Jess would kick him in the boy bits again. But Jason being Jason, he'd had to find someone else to bully. And that person was Rex.

'Did your last school kick you out for being a jack-up weirdo?' Jason said.

Rex's face went bright red as he looked down at his ankles. 'We moved.'

'Everything was going fine until you came here.'

'Apart from the PALS stuff,' someone shouted, and a few people laughed.

'I haven't done anything,' Rex said. 'I don't even know where you live.'

'I'm Jason Newbold: everyone in this school knows where I live. And someone set fire to my house.'

Jess marched forward and put herself in between Jason and Rex. 'Why would Rex set fire to your house? He hasn't even been here long enough to know how much of a jerk you are.'

'Oooh, burn,' I said. I totally had Jess's back.

'Stay out of this, freak girl,' Jason said, but more quietly and while moving his hands to cover his 'area'. 'Should have known you'd stick up for this scuzzy tramp.'

'Should we go in?' I whispered to Dave.

'Nah – Jess has it covered, and she'll be mad at you for thinking she couldn't handle it.'

'Call me that again, Jason,' she said, her eyes narrowing. She took a step closer to him.

'Whatever,' he said, edging back. 'Just stay the hell away from me – all of you weirdos. And when I find out who set my house on fire, they're dead.'

'Teachers coming!' someone said, and the group started to break up, leaving only me, Dave, Jess and Rex.

'Are you OK, mate?' Dave said to Rex.

Rex said nothing but looked like he might cry. There were only two situations in Year 6 when it was acceptable to cry: one – if you received a potentially life-threatening injury, for example, if someone smashed a chair over your head or you got a really bad paper cut; two – if you failed one of your exams and had to spend the next month in intervention. If he started crying now, it would be totally awkward. And I felt a bit sorry for him.

'Do you want to sit with us?' I said, and Jess smiled at me for the first time in a week.

'Thanks, but I want to be on my own right now,' Rex sniffed.

At that moment, Miss Hussein reached us. 'Is everything OK, guys?'

'Rex is having a tough day,' Dave said.

'I'm sorry to hear that, Rex,' Miss Hussein smiled at him. And not like a Miss Smilie smile; it was a gentle, rosy smile with a twinkle in it. 'Would you like to come inside for a bit and have some quiet time? I think there might be some ginger biscuits left over from lunch – we could sneak you a few and find you a book in the library.'

Rex nodded and started walking towards the door.

'Thank you for looking after him,' Miss Hussein twinkled at us. 'It's so hard being new and it makes me proud when I see people like you being kind. I owe you all a ginger biscuit, too.' She hurried to catch up with Rex.

'There's definitely something sinister about her,' I said.

Jess rolled her eyes. 'Come on, let's go back to our bench.'

'Maybe she set fire to Jason's house?' I said.

Jess and Dave both turned to look at me. You know you've gone too far when even Darth Daver gives you the stink eye.

'I know, I know. Miss Hussein is like a fluffy unicorn and I'm being stupid and desperate. It's just that I want a new mission so badly.'

'I heard Marek saying the fire happened when Jason's Xbox blew up,' Jess said. 'It was just an accident.'

'Wow – he gamed so hard he blew up his Xbox!'

I pictured a giant explosion with Jason's family leaping out of the way in slow motion, flames twenty metres high and a mushroom cloud of smoke where Jason's house used to be.

'I think it was just a small fire,' Dave said, as though he could see right into my mind. 'Nobody got hurt but one of the curtains was a bit brown at the bottom.'

How disappointing.

'Well, at least one good thing came out of this,' I said.

'You actually thought about someone else other than yourself for a change?' said Jess.

'Calm down, Saint Jessticles – even your hair looks ragey. Anyway, you got more out of this situation than anyone.'

'Why's that?' We'd reached the bench and she stopped and turned, hands on hips.

'Because Rex is definitely going to get you a job in the animal sanctuary now.'

She sighed and turned away, but not before I saw the corner of her mouth twitch upwards in what looked like the start of a smile.

We sat back down on the Reflection Bench.

'Well, that was the most action we've seen in a while,' Dave said.

A horrid feeling swept over me. I felt heavy and sad and it was hard to take a breath – kind of like I was being sucked down a plughole. After everything we'd been through and all we achieved. How had life got so boring?

'I can't stand this,' I said. 'No secret missions. No psychotic villains. No life or death situations. Life sucks right now.'

'The Professor gave us our powers for a reason, Alex,' said Jess, 'and we did what we needed to do. We won. We should be happy.'

'Then why aren't I?' It was true that Miss

Fortress, a.k.a. The Professor, had given us our powers specifically to stop Miss Smilie, but that didn't mean we shouldn't use them for other cool things. Ten years old was too young to retire.

A loud rustling from the cherry tree branches over our heads made us all look up, and a familiar-looking grey blob swooped towards us.

'Dexter!' Jess and I jumped up and shouted at the same time, before remembering we shouldn't be drawing attention to the fact that we had a friend who's a pigeon. We hadn't seen him since the day of Miss Smilie's arrest and, honestly, I'd never been so happy to see his beady eyes and yucky toe stump.

He landed on the bench next to us and started strutting back and forth like a boss.

Jess launched into the series of jerky movements that meant she was listening to Dexter and, it could have been my imagination, but I reckon she was doing it with more enthusiasm than I'd seen from her in weeks.

'Like what, though?' Jess was saying, and I felt this rising excitement, like the opposite of being sucked down a plughole. Maybe something completely awesome was going to happen.

When Jess stopped twitching, Dexter turned to me, bobbed his head and then took off.

'Did you see that?' I said. 'He nodded at me! He doesn't hate me anymore!'

'I saw him move his head a tiny bit,' said Jess. 'I wouldn't call it a nod, exactly.'

'Shush, Jessticles, it was totally a nod – a mark of respect between comrades. He was practically telling me he loves me.'

A slimy wet poo suddenly fell from the sky and spattered on the bench next to me.

Dave cracked up.

'I don't think it's love just yet, Alex,' said Jess.

'It wasn't on my head, so I'll take it.' I would not let her chill my buzz. 'Anyway, what did he say? Is it a mission? IS IT A MISSION?'

'I wouldn't call it a mission,' she sighed. 'But he said he's been witnessing some funny business on the ground. He made it clear to The Prof that something was bothering him, and she told him to pass the intel on to us.'

'What funny business, Jess? Tell me!' I bounced up and down on the bench.

'It's the animals. The animals are acting out of sorts; doing things they shouldn't be. We need to provide The Professor with a report.'

'Jess, my delightful friend, do you know what this is?'

'It's not a mission.'

'IT'S A MISSION!'

'Not really.'

'It's a mission, isn't it, Dave?' I turned to him for help.

'It does sound a bit missiony,' he smiled.

Jess whacked him on the arm. 'Now he'll be unbearable.'

'Mission, mission, mission,' I marched around the bench chanting.

'Shut up, Alex,' Jess said.

'Do you know what, Jessticles?' I stopped in front of her and leaned in. 'Mission.'

Jess rubbed her face with her hands and sighed. 'I told you, Dave.'

# 3

## The Really Surprising
## Sanctuary

So the next day was Jess's first shift at the animal sanctuary. Well, I say Jess's first shift, but it was actually my first shift, too. We'd spoken (argued) about it after Dexter's exciting revelation and decided (reluctantly agreed) that it would make sense for both of us to be there in order to conduct the most thorough investigation of the strange animal behaviour. I really didn't want to be getting scratched or to clean up poo, or whatever it is people do at animal sanctuaries, but I am a professional agent, and the mission comes first. To be honest, I don't think Jess wanted me there, ruining her little fantasy world, but we both just had to deal with it. We work best as a team.

My mum agreed that me and Jess could walk to the sanctuary together after school, as it wasn't very far and she'd finally given me my very own shiny new phone. Obvs I had to promise to text her when I left school, and text her when I got safely to the sanctuary, and text her if anything happened, and all that, but it was my first step towards freedom, so I didn't complain too much.

'Where is Cherry Tree Lane Animal Sanctuary?' I asked Jess as we walked out of the school gate.

'Are you kidding?' She looked across at me and rolled her eyes.

'Is that a trick question?'

'Was your question a trick question?' she said.

'Why would my question be a trick question?' This was a confusing conversation.

'Because it was a completely stupid question.'

'In what way was it stupid, my stroppy sidekick?'

'Alex,' she huffed, 'it's called Cherry Tree Lane Animal Sanctuary.'

'So?'

'Why do you think it's called that?'

'I don't know. Everything around here is called Cherry Tree Lane something or other.' Still confused.

'Maybe because they're all on Cherry Tree Lane?' She was looking straight ahead so I couldn't really see her expression, but I could hear in her voice that it was one of disgust. Which was totally unfair.

'Listen, Jessticles. I've lived around here my whole life, and been at Cherry Tree Lane Primary for even longer. I think I'd know if there was an animal sanctuary on Cherry Tree Lane.' That told her. 'Why have you stopped walking?'

'Because we're here, Double-O-Dufus.'

We were standing in front of a gate in the middle of a crumbly wall. The gate was green, although half the paint was peeling off, and it had a black handle and a sign that said, Cherry Tree Lane Animal Sanctuary, with a picture of a hedgehog. The nails on the sign were rusty and the gateposts were covered in vines, like they'd been growing there for a hundred years.

I side-eyed Jess. 'It must be new.'

Jess reached for the handle but before she could turn it, the door creaked open and someone walked right into us.

'I'm so sorry!' the guy said. 'I wasn't expecting anyone to be coming in.'

'Don't worry,' Jess said, gazing up at him. 'It wasn't your fault.'

'Well, technically it was,' I said, but Jess jabbed me in the ribs.

The guy laughed. He was older than us, but not old enough to be, like, a teacher or a dad. Anyway, his hair was too cool for him to be either of those. It was that not-too-long and not-too-short, messy but not-messy hair that I tried to make mine go like. He was tallish, wearing skinny jeans, a band T-shirt and a cardigan with some badges on it. One of them said 'Vegan Warrior'.

'I love your badge,' Jess said, looking more impressed than I'd ever seen her. And, as if he wasn't perfect enough already, a German Shepherd dog pushed out from behind him and licked Jess's hand.

'Settle down, Meena,' the guy said. 'Some people are anxious around big dogs.'

'It's fine – I love animals.' Jess knelt down and

made a fuss of Meena. I expected her to start twitching, as she often did around dogs because she couldn't help talking to them. But she didn't twitch, she just rubbed Meena's head and smiled up at Mr Vegan Dog-Lover.

'So I'm guessing you're the new volunteers.' When he smiled, he got these dimples in his cheeks and his eyes shone like melted chocolate. 'Nice to meet you. I'm Taran.'

'I'm Jess,' Jess sparkled back at him. 'Lovely to meet you, too.'

'Ahem,' I coughed.

'This is Alex,' Jess said.

I opened my mouth to speak but I didn't get a chance...

'Do you work at the sanctuary?' Jess asked.

'Sort of. I'm a specialist in animal behaviour and I work with most of the rescue centres, vets and refuges in the area. They call me in if they need my so-called expertise.' Taran smiled again in an embarrassed way.

It was like a brag without being a brag. He was good.

'That's so interesting,' said Jess. 'I'd like to do something like that when I go to uni.'

I was going to point out that as Jess had only just turned eleven, it was ridiculous to be planning that far ahead, but I couldn't get a word in.

'You must love it,' she said to Taran.

'I do,' Taran said. 'I'm such a lucky guy to be able to work with animals every day. I've loved them all my life, been a vegan since I was six and decided to dedicate my life to helping them at about the same age. Four years at university and here I am, living the dream.'

Jess's face turned into the heart eyes emoji, but I was distracted. Taran had lied, but I couldn't work out which part of what he'd said wasn't true. I wanted to ask him some questions, but Jess suddenly noticed the smell and got all flustered.

'We'd better go in or we're going to be late,' she said, jumping up and trying to manoeuvre Taran away from the stink. Meena tapped at Jess's leg with her paw, so Jess bent down to stroke her again. 'Lovely to meet you, Meena.'

'Hopefully see you again, sometime,' Taran called as he walked away. 'Good luck with your new job.'

'Thank you,' Jess waved. 'Bye, Taran. Bye, Meena.'

I looked at her. 'Er, what the heck was that?'

'Why did you have to have your ear switched on?' she said, obviously annoyed with me for some reason.

'We're on a mission, Jessticles. When I'm on a mission, I keep my ear ready for action at all times. Why didn't you switch on the twitch?'

'There was no need,' Jess said. 'Besides, it's our first day and he works here – I didn't want to risk him thinking we're nuts.'

'Mmmhmm,' I said.

'Shut up, Alex.' She pushed the gate open and we walked through. Behind it was an overgrown path that led to a house that matched the crumbly wall and the ancient gate. Rex was standing at the front door.

'You're late. Here's your overalls,' he said, shoving green bundles at me and Jess.

'Thanks,' Jess said, holding hers up so that it unfolded into some kind of material that matched the wall, the gate and the house.

'Is this a type of clothes?' I had to ask because I wasn't entirely sure.

'They're overalls,' Jess hissed. 'The same as Rex is wearing.'

'Put them on,' Rex said, and stood there while we shoved them over our uniforms. I made them look swag, just FYI.

'So,' I said. 'Do you like Cherry Tree Lane so far?'

'Not really.'

'How come you moved here?'

'They were looking for someone to take over this place,' he shrugged. 'Mum wanted to.'

'Cool,' I said. 'Cool, cool.'

Rex led us through a narrow passage to a large room at the back of the house. Before he even opened the door, the noise hit me like an attack on my ears. Followed by the smell like a spear up the nose.

'Oh jeez,' I said, covering my face with my sleeve, which didn't help at all because the sleeve smelt just as bad.

'Now you know what it's like to hang out with you,' Jess said.

Beyond the door was a large room full of hutches, tanks and enclosures, and about a million different kinds of animal, most of them barking or grunting or squeaking. At one end of the room there was a separated area, like a small kitchen.

'Ooh, snacks!' I said, half running towards it because the long walk from school had made me super-hungry.

On the counter, where the cakes and sausage rolls should be, there was a metal board and the biggest knife I'd ever seen. The board was covered in red stuff and bits of fluff. I couldn't work out what it was. Next to the board was a bowl, and inside…

'OMG – entrails!' I did a little sick in my mouth. 'With pieces of beak and foot.'

'Help yourself, we have plenty,' a voice came from the other end of the room.

I turned to see a person who was really short but somehow large at the same time. It had long hair, a dark reddish colour but with stripes of grey, and was wearing what looked like five different holey cardigans on top of each other. It seemed to be a lady, except for the hair all over her face.

'This is my mum,' Rex said.

'Nice to meet you, Mrs Rex's mum,' I said, edging away from the chopped-up bird snacks in case she tried to make me eat them. 'Jess,' I whispered. 'She has a beard.'

'That's a chinchilla, Alex.'

'A chin warmer, surely?'

'No, a chinchilla. It's an animal.'

And Mrs Rex's mum's beard suddenly disappeared round the back of her neck.

'Rex!' Rex's mum called. 'Come!'

Rex trotted over to her immediately.

'Good boy,' she said and patted him on the head.

Me and Jess raised eyebrows at each other.

'As a rule, I don't allow outsiders into the sanctuary.' She gave us both a sharp look. 'We don't like strangers poking into our business or upsetting the babies.'

I tried to look around the room without looking like I was looking, wondering where she was keeping the babies.

'But I understand that you helped my boy, and that you at least...' (she turned to Jess) '...know your way around a rodent.'

I couldn't help it, a little snigger slipped out.

'Let me make this perfectly clear,' Rex's mum said. 'You are here on a trial basis. If you cause distress in this sanctum, or if you attempt to lead my son astray and undo my years of training with him, you will be banished. Is that understood?'

'Yes ma'am,' I said, and almost saluted but thought it might annoy her even more, so turned it into a forehead scratch. Styling it out as always.

'We won't let you down,' said Jess.

'Show them around, Rex, and give them precise instructions,' Rex's mum said. 'And none of you are to enter my office, under any circumstances.'

'What's in your office?' I said. Jess kicked me in the shin.

'It is forbidden!' Mrs Rex shouted. Then she put her fingers in her mouth and made this really loud, high whistle. Rex walked quickly to a sliding door at the back of the room while Mrs Rex left the way we came in.

'Did she just whistle to him?' Jess said so only I could hear. 'Like a sheepdog?'

'I know, she put her fingers in her mouth and she'd just been touching that chinchilla. So gross.'

We followed Rex around the sanctuary, which was much bigger on the inside than it looked from the front. There were three animal rooms in the house itself, two of them filled with small sick and injured animals, and the other one with all sorts of freaky creatures, like snakes and tarantulas.

'The reptile room needs to be kept secure,' Rex grunted. 'These animals shouldn't be loose, and some of them are good at escaping. Especially that one,' he pointed at a large orange snake curled up in a tank.

Rex led us outside, where there was a big shed-slash-barn thing, next to some fenced-off grassy areas that had donkeys and a tiny horse inside.

'Are any of the reptiles loose right now?' I said, looking into the enclosure where the horse was jumping around like it was having some kind of psychotic episode.

'Scared of snakes?' Jess raised an eyebrow at me.

'I'm more scared of that deranged horse,' I said. 'Do horses normally do that?'

'Harry does,' Rex shrugged. 'Just don't get too close to his hooves. He kicks.'

We carried on past the field and I swear the horse was laughing. Personally, I didn't see what there was to laugh about – I'd just signed up to work in a den of dangerous beasts. There was also a pond with ducks and a vicious-looking swan with a bandaged-up wing, and a few other enclosures that looked suspiciously calm and empty. Who knows what was in those.

Rex gave us lots of information in as few words as humanly possible, but to be honest I didn't take much of it in. I'd switched into agent mode.

'So, Rex,' I said, 'how are the animals here?'

'Some of them are brought in by members of the public. Some we find ourselves.'

'That's super-interesting, but I meant how are they feeling?'

He looked at me like I was mental. 'It depends.'

'On what?'

'There's a deer here that got hit by a truck. She's not doing too good.'

'How awful!' Jess gasped. 'Can I see her? Maybe I can help?'

'You a deer expert?' Rex said.

'Well, no, but...'

'She needs to be kept quiet. Me and Mum only.'

I was getting impatient. 'But what about the other animals? The ones who aren't half dead?'

'Alex!' Jess glared at me. It was like she'd forgotten why we were here.

I ignored her. 'Are they all acting normally? Are they happy?'

Rex gave me a hard look. 'Yeah,' he said. 'I s'pose.'

A vibration stirred deep in the right side of my head, gathering momentum as it pushed through my ear canal, resulting in a loud, angry fart. I knew Jess and Rex couldn't hear it, but a fart that size was definitely going to be a real stinker. Even surrounded by animal droppings, it stood out.

Jess sniffed and side-eyed me.

Rex lifted his foot and checked for poo. 'We need to get to work – you can start by feeding. Here's a list of the pens and what needs to go where. I'll be close by at all times.'

He gave Jess a tatty piece of paper and walked over to an egg incubator. (FYI – these are quite like the ones in Pokemon Go, except they can hold more than one egg at a time and they hatch birds, not little monsters.)

I nudged Jess. 'He lied about the animals!'

'Yeah, I figured.'

'But why would he lie? And what is he hiding?'

'I don't know, but we can't talk about this now. He'll hear us.'

'It seems to me, Jessticles, that you're more worried about helping these sick and injured animals than you are about our mission,' I said. 'Where are your priorities?'

She gave me a metal bowl of meaty-looking jelly stuff. 'Take this to enclosure 17. And it says on the instructions to make sure the animal is actually eating it before you leave. Apparently he has bad eyesight and a damaged sense of smell, so you need to help him find the food.'

I carried the bowl outside, wondering what had happened to this animal to make it blind and… What's the word for not being able to smell properly? Like deaf but for smells. Let's call it smeaf. I thought about what it would be like to be mostly blind and mostly smeaf and it seemed to me that I was pretty lucky to have all my senses functioning well, even if it meant I had to look at Jess's stroppy face, and listen to her nagging, and smell all the weird vegan foods she ate. A bit of brown juice from the bowl dripped on to my finger and I wiped it on my overalls. The animal wasn't missing out in this case – it smelt horrid.

Enclosure 17 was about the size of my bedroom, and full of grass and wild-looking plants. In one corner there was a little wooden house with a small round doorway that had bits of straw poking out of it. I assumed that whatever animal this food was for would be inside the house. As you probably know, I'm usually Luke Skywalker brave, but I'd had a bit of trouble with animals in the past – they didn't always like me that much – so I was nervous. I put the bowl down on the grass outside the hut and gently tapped on the roof.

'Helloooo, your dinner's ready,' I called, in what I hoped was a gentle voice. 'And also, please don't bite me.'

There was a rustling in the box and a pointy snout with a tiny wet black nose emerged from the straw, sniffing into the air. The sniffing thing doesn't usually work out that well for me, so I stepped back and sat on an old log.

The snout moved forwards in jerky movements and I could see two black eyes, one bright, and the other one kind of clouded over. Fluffy brown ears followed, then two paws and the rest of the body, which was small and round and covered in brown fluff and blonde and brown spikes. I don't know much about hedgehogs, but it looked harmless, and actually quite cute.

'Hello, little guy,' I said, and the hedgehog's nose quivered in my direction. I wondered exactly how damaged his sense of smell was, and whether he'd be grossed out by me like most other animals are. He walked towards me of his own free will, as though he was actually interested to meet me. I picked up a chunk of food. It was slimy and disgusting, but I wanted to try something. I held my hand out flat, like I'd seen Rex do with the guinea pig, and put the food on my palm. The hedgehog sniffed me once more and then climbed on to my hand and licked the food with his tongue. I could feel his claws on my skin, but it didn't hurt – it felt kind of nice. He ate the chunk of meat and nudged my wrist with his nose. So I did something I never thought I'd do – I put both my hands flat, picked him up and lifted him close to my face. I figured he was blind in that cloudy eye and I thought he might want a closer look at me.

At first he curled up into a ball, his prickles crisscrossing and digging into my hands.

'It's OK,' I said. 'I won't hurt you. Have some more food.'

I dropped another lump of meat into the place where his face hidden. He made a noise like a soft huff, and sucked the food in. Then he poked out his snout, peeped at me through his good eye, and licked the tip of my nose. I know this is going to sound proper soft, but it was the most adorable thing that had ever happened to me.

'What's your name, buddy?' I said. 'My friend Jess would be able to tell me but she's inside, so I'm going to call you Mr Prickles, just until I can find out what your real name is. I hope that's OK?'

Mr Prickles made a snuffly noise, crawled on to my shoulder and nuzzled his face into my neck. The ear-flap from my hat protected my skin from his spikes, so it didn't hurt. And for the first time in my life, I understood why Jess loved animals so much.

'Are you happy here, Mr Prickles?' I said.

'Why wouldn't it be happy here?' Rex's voice seemed to come out of nowhere.

I looked around as he sort of materialised out of some bushes like the flipping Indominus rex out of Jurassic World.

'Do you have inbuilt cloaking technology or something, Rex?'

'I told you I'd be close by at all times.'

'It's lucky I'm always alert then. You could have made a less courageous person jump out of their skin.'

I couldn't work Rex out. He seemed more unhappy than evil, but he was strange and defensive, and of course there was the lying.

'Why did you ask the hedgehog if it's happy?'

'Just making conversation, Rex. He looked like he wanted a chat.' I gave him a hard look, as suggested in the Awesome Agent Alex Academy handbook. I'd practised it in the mirror a bunch of times, so I knew it was pretty intimidating. 'Why wouldn't you want me to ask him that?'

'Hedgehogs can't talk.'

'Good point – let me rephrase the question: why are you bothered about me being bothered about whether or not Mr ... I mean the hedgehog is happy?'

'Because the hedgehog is fine. The animals here are well looked after and have no reason to be unhappy.'

It was the most I'd ever heard Rex say and it made Mr Prickles huff. I'd found since I got my power, that if you make people really annoyed, they often slip up and tell you more than they intended. And in this case, it was a masterstroke, because my ear rumbled and a stink spread through the air. Mr Prickles, who got the full force of it being nestled on my shoulder, didn't seem to mind. He just sniffed at my ear, which felt all tickly and nice.

'Of course they are,' I said. I didn't want to pee Rex off too much in case he fired me before I could find out what was going on. 'I meant is he happy here in England. I believe hedgehogs come from the South American rainforest originally, so I thought it might be a bit cold for him.'

'Hedgehogs are native to Britain,' Rex said, giving me the look I'd seen so many times on so many faces, especially Jess's. Some people might have thought it meant 'you are a moron', but I preferred to think of it as 'your skill at mind games is both confusing and impressive at the same time.'

'That's what they want you to think,' I said.

'There are other animals that need feeding. Put the hedgehog down.' Rex started walking towards the house.

'Wait,' I said. 'He's not going to do that long winter-sleeping thing, is he?' I said. I didn't like the thought of not being able to see Mr Prickles until spring.

'Hedgehogs need to be at least six hundred and

fifty grams to hibernate, and that one is only about four hundred. He wouldn't survive.'

Rex walked off. I didn't know how he could be so un-bothered at the thought of Mr Prickles not surviving.

'I wish I could take you home, Mr Prickles,' I said. 'I have to go now, but I'll come back and see you tomorrow. And make sure you don't hibernate.'

I carefully lifted him off my shoulder and put him on the ground near his bowl. He looked at me and squeaked and then carried on eating. As I walked away, I turned back for one last look at him, and I swear he was looking back.

# 4

## Confession Time

Rex and his mum kept us really busy for the rest of the time we were at the sanctuary, and Rex never left us alone, so me and Jess couldn't talk. It was dark by the time we'd finished, so my mum insisted on picking us up. It started pouring with rain on the way back and, by the time we'd got home, there was a massive storm going on. I hoped Mr Prickles was OK. Mum wanted to hear all about the animal sanctuary, so she made Jess stay for dinner and we had to eat at the dining table with my whole family. So annoying. But at least Mum had finally got it into her head that Jess wouldn't eat sausages like the rest of us. She kept this packet of stuff in the freezer that supposedly looked and tasted exactly the same as meat, but was made from mushroom or something. It was a weird grey colour and smelt funny, but Jess seemed happy enough.

'I have to tell you something, Jess,' I said, as soon as we were on our own.

'Me too.' She pulled out a stool at our breakfast bar and sat down, her teeny legs dangling so that she looked like a hobbit sitting on a giant's chair.

'Me first, though – me first!' I'd been thinking about it for the whole of dinner and I just had to get it out.

'Fine,' she said. 'Is it to do with the investigation? What did you find out?'

'Oh.' I bit my lip and tried to look like a serious agent. 'It's sort of about the investigation.'

'What is it?' Jess frowned at me, and suddenly I felt a bit silly.

'Jess. I met someone.'

'Right,' she said. 'Who did you meet? And how is this about the investigation?'

An A-grade agent always thinks on his feet and, luckily, I came up with an amazing plan.

'His name is Mr Prickles,' I said. 'And he's going to be our informant.'

'And Mr Prickles is?' Jess raised an eyebrow and sniffed the air.

'A hedgehog, of course,' I snorted.

'How do you know his name is Mr Prickles?' she said. 'Was he wearing a badge?'

'Er, no. I discussed it with him and we agreed that would be his agent name.'

'You can talk to animals now, too?'

'Not in the way you can, Jessticles. But we communicated in other ways.'

'Such as?'

'Snuffles, nuzzles and nose kisses.'

'Alex,' Jess turned to me, her eyes wide, 'have you fallen in love with a hedgehog?'

It sounded stupid, I know, but... 'I can't help it! He's the most adorable little dude in the world! We just totally got each other from the moment we met.'

'I so did not see this coming,' Jess said, clearly trying not to laugh.

'I really want you to meet him – you'll totally understand when you see him for yourself.'

Jess was looking at me in this strange way that I'd never seen before.

'Now I feel a bit silly,' I said.

'Don't you dare!' she said. 'This is great, Alex. You're usually awful with animals – totally insensitive and rude. I'm so proud of you!'

'Really?' I said.

'Really,' she nodded. And I knew she wasn't lying.

'Thanks, Jess,' I said. 'I've never felt this way about any animal before.'

'Alex…' she said.

'It's just that I don't usually like them very much. They're just there, you know, doing their own thing and not being at all loveable.'

'Alex!' Jess gave me a nudge with her elbow – I thought in a 'go on' kind of way.

'Mr Prickles is different from any other animal I've ever met.'

'ALEX!' Jess kicked me hard in the leg (again) and pointed to the end of the breakfast bar.

I turned to see what she was pointing at.

'Oh…' I said. This was awkward. 'Hi, Bob. Hi, Elle.'

Bob was eyeballing me through the glass wall

of his tank. And he did not look happy. In the tank next door, Elle was doing the same. Have you ever seen a goldfish glare? Well, it's pretty harsh, I can tell you, and I was getting a double whammy.

'When I said all that stuff just now, about not liking animals and Mr Prickles being the best animal ever, I should make it clear that I absolutely knew you were listening, and I assumed that you realised that I … when I say "animal", I'm meaning only creatures with legs and fur.'

It's lucky that the smell of fart doesn't pass through water.

'How are you two doing today, anyway?' I said. 'Have you got any further with your plans?'

Bob and Elle were planning to move in together, which was a massive deal for Bob because he'd only ever lived alone and he was kind of fussy about things. He spent a couple of days in the school aquarium once, during our PALS mission, and the chaos and disorder stressed him out really badly. So before he'd share a tank, he was insisting on planning every tiny detail: the colour and arrangement of the gravel at the bottom; the placement of any furnishings;

a daily schedule for them both to follow. Personally, I thought it was nuts, but Elle seemed to understand and she was being very patient about the whole thing.

Jess started twitching away by the tank, so I got myself a drink. When Bob explains things, it always takes a while.

'They can't agree on whose tank they should move into,' Jess said at last. 'Elle says she can't live in Bob's because it's too minimalist and cold, and Bob says Elle's tank is full of clutter and tat.'

'Can't they put Elle's stuff into one half of Bob's tank?' I said. 'Or clear out half of Elle's so Bob can move in there?'

Bob's response to my suggestion was to turn his tail on me and swim away in disgust. Elle's was to flick a piece of gravel against the wall of her tank.

'I guess not,' I said.

The rain was falling really hard, thundering on the roof like pebbles were being thrown from the International Space Station. It was the perfect weather for terrible things to happen: a murder, a kidnapping, an argument between two fish and a human.

'So I should tell you what I found out at the

animal sanctuary,' said Jess. 'You know, on the mission that you were annoyingly excited about and now seem to have forgotten.'

'Not forgotten,' I said. 'A good agent always plays his cards close to his chest. I just wanted to make you think I'd forgotten.'

My ear farted and Jess screwed up her nose. 'Right. Anyway, I couldn't speak to the animals because Rex was there the whole time and I didn't want to give us away or get us fired. If I'd asked any questions, he would have heard me.'

'Good thinking, Agent Nutcracker.'

'But I managed to listen to a few creatures when Rex wasn't looking.'

'Did they say that Rex and his mum are the biggest weirdos ever?' I said. 'That's totally what I'd be saying if I had to be around them all the time.'

'No, although the way she spoke to him was a bit odd.'

'A bit odd? She treated him like he was her dog!'

'Yeah,' Jess said, although I could tell she hated to agree with me. 'It made me feel a bit uncomfortable.'

'A bit uncomfortable! I wanted to poke myself in both eyes so I wouldn't be able to see them.'

'The whistle was a bit much.'

'A bit much? It was lock-you-up-in-a-special-hospital bonkers!'

'Stop repeating everything I say in the form of a question-slash-exclamation,' Jess huffed. 'It's annoying.'

'Well then, stop trying to turn big things into small things. This is an investigation, Jessticles – we need to see things clearly.'

'Fine – it was awful, OK? Rex and his mum have a disturbing relationship and I never ever want to see them interacting with each other again!'

A crack of thunder boomed in my ears, and at the same time a lightning flash turned the room bright white for a second.

'Bit harsh, Jess,' I said.

Jess's face turned pink and she looked like she was going to thump me.

'So if the animals weren't talking about Rex and his trainer,' I said. 'What were they saying?'

'They were scared,' she said. 'They kept saying, "We must hide or he will find us!"'

'Who will find them? I said.

'Someone called The Rattler.'

'The Rattler?' I said. 'That's the name of a horror-movie psychopath if ever I've heard one. This mission just got a whole lot darker.'

Another crash of thunder roared across the sky, so loud that the breakfast bar shook and glasses and plates clinked in the cupboards. And then all the lights went out.

As you know, I'm a bad-A agent, so the lights going out suddenly in the middle of a storm, when we were discussing a creepily named psycho-villain, didn't even make me flinch. Or even if I did a tiny bit, nobody would have seen because it was so dark. Not even, like, in the house at night dark when there are still specks of light coming from the streetlight outside, or a car driving past, or from the TV where you've left it on standby. It was the darkest, blackest dark I had ever seen.

'What happened?' Jess's voice came out of the darkness.

'There can only be one explanation,' I said. 'The Rattler knows we're on to him and has come to silence us permanently. Feel around for a weapon, Jess – we're going to have to fight for our lives.'

'Alex! Jess!' My mum's voice called from somewhere in the house. 'Don't worry, it's just a power cut. Half the town is out!'

'Or, you know, that's a possibility, too,' I said.

I think I actually heard Jess's eyes roll. It was like the noise you'd get if you pulled apart two pieces of bread covered in sticky honey.

Once Mum set up a few candles and torches, and I brought my lightsaber collection down from my room, we had enough light to see each other at least. Jess spent the next thirty minutes twitching because Bob's pump was off and he was worried about an algae infestation. It didn't leave us much time to plan.

'I need some time alone with the animals at the sanctuary,' Jess said. 'How can we get Rex and his mum to leave?'

'It would have to be something drastic,' I said. 'I'm pretty sure Rex doesn't trust me.'

'Well, that's a surprise.'

'Remember Rex said they sometimes have to go out to collect injured animals? We need to have a fake callout – some animal emergency that needs both of them and that's super-urgent so they have no choice but to leave us.'

'That's not a bad idea,' Jess said, 'But we can't do it ourselves – it needs to be anonymous. If they think it's us, they'll never let us in the sanctuary again.'

'We can't ask Darth Daver. It has to be a grown-up or they'll be suspicious.'

We looked at each other.

'Miss Fortress!'

# 5

## Criminal Squirrels and Medium-sized Sheep

'So all you have to do is call this number and tell them that you've come across a seriously injured animal,' I said.

'Like a rabbit?' Miss Fortress swallowed a mouthful of coffee.

'No, it has to be something bigger – something that would need both Rex and his mum to collect it. It has to be a two-person job.'

'A cow?'

'Too big, Miss Fortress,' Jess said. 'It would take more than two people to carry a cow.'

'Then what?' For someone who was supposed to be a scientific genius, Miss Fortress was absolutely useless at this type of thing. You'd never believe she was The Professor who gave us our powers.

'A sheep,' I said. 'A medium-sized one.'

'So you need me to call this number and tell them that I have discovered a seriously injured medium-sized sheep?'

'Exactly,' I said.

'You might need to give them a few details about the injury,' said Jess. 'You could say that it looks like it has a broken leg. Then they would need two people to lift it.'

'And say it's bleeding,' I added. 'You know, to make it more of an emergency.'

'And where have I supposedly found this medium-sized sheep who appears to have a broken leg and is bleeding?' Miss Fortress pushed her hair back off her face, making even more of a mess of it.

'It needs to be quite a way away from the sanctuary,' Jess said, 'so it will take them a while to get there.'

'But not so far that it would fall into another sanctuary's jurisdiction,' I said. 'I expect they have boundaries, don't they, like the police?'

'Why does everything you two ask me to do get ridiculously complicated?' Miss Fortress sighed.

'You could always go to the sanctuary and ask the animals about The Rattler yourself,' said Jess, hands on hips and doing one of her looks.

'No need for the attitude, Miss Lawler. I am your teacher and I can still keep you in at lunch, you know.'

'Let's focus, shall we?' It was lucky I always kept a calm head in these situations. I just needed to ooze my usual charm. 'We need you to do this, Hope. May I call you Hope?'

'Certainly not!' Miss Fortress slammed her mug down on her desk. 'But I'll make the call if it will help your investigation. Dexter has been anxious this past week, and if he thinks there's an issue with the animals then I'm certain there is something untoward occurring.'

'Thanks, Miss. There's so much untowardness happening, we defos need your help,' I said.

'What I don't understand is how this "The Rattler" is connected with the strange animal behaviour that Dexter's been witnessing outside the sanctuary. Have you seen the news reports?'

'We don't know if they're connected,' Jess said. 'But seeing as you decided to electric shock our brains, without our permission, to give us powers to help you with *your* thing, the least you can do is back us up on this. We want to help at the sanctuary.'

'What news reports?' I said.

'Every day there are people on the news harping on about strange occurrences in the natural world. Animal experts coming up with obscure theories.' Miss Fortress tipped the last drops of coffee into her mouth. 'Like those blasted foxes. Have you heard those unearthly noises? All night, every night. I have to drink coffee just to get me through the day.'

'But the fox noise only started a couple of weeks ago, Miss,' I said. 'You've been drinking coffee forever.'

'And the squirrel attacks,' she said.

'What squirrel attacks?' said Jess, looking up from picking her nails.

'For goodness' sake – don't you children know what's going on outside your own tiny, self-obsessed lives?'

'Er, no?' I said.

'Squirrels have been mugging people.' Miss Fortress put down her cup and opened a desk drawer. 'Attacking people on the streets and stealing their phones.'

'Wait – what?' I couldn't believe what I was hearing.

'They leap from trees, kicking and scratching, and knock people's electronic devices out of their hands,' she said.

'That sounds crazy,' said Jess.

'That sounds awesome,' I said. 'Ninja squirrels.'

'It's a serious matter,' Miss Fortress said.

'We'll make sure we watch the news more often,' Jess said. 'And I'll ask the animals at the sanctuary if they know what's going on outside.'

'We'll probably need to speak to some others, too – animals outside the sanctuary. I wonder if we can get our hands on a squirrel?'

'We won't be able to catch a squirrel, Alex,' Jess frowned at me.

'Not with that attitude, Jessticles. As it happens, I have an awesome plan for catching squirrels. All we need is a dustpan and brush, an old sock, some pebbles and a pink ribbon.'

'Please don't tell me your plan is to make a girl squirrel and use it to lure in a boy squirrel?' Jess sighed.

'Of course not,' I said. My ear farted and the smell was like mouldy chicken.

Jess raised both eyebrows at me.

'Fine, maybe that is my plan,' I said. 'It always works in cartoons.'

'For the millionth time, Double-O-Dopey, cartoons are not the same as real life!'

'For goodness sake, you two, you're giving me a headache!' Miss Fortress snapped. 'Get out of my classroom this instant.'

Me and Jess walked out as quickly as we could. Miss Fortress was about to blow.

'You'll still make the call for us, though, right?' I said, poking my head back through the door. 'In a few days, when Rex and his mum will trust us enough to leave us in the sanctuary?'

'Out!'

Something crashed into the wall next to me. It was Miss Fortress's signed picture of the guy who played Bane in the Batman movie, except he was holding a puppy and not wearing the cool mask.

'I'll take that as a yes,' I said. 'By the way, Miss, you're so inappropriate.'

I ran before she could throw anything else at me.


Every day that week crawled by as we waited for school to finish so we could go back to the animal sanctuary. I was excited about carrying out our plan. I was desperate to get some more information on The Rattler. Most of all, I loved spending time with Mr Prickles.

On our fifth day heading towards the sanctuary, we bumped into Rex at the school gate. Jason, Kyle and Ronnie were walking behind him and throwing bits of twig at his back. They were bouncing off his backpack but, from the look on his face, I could tell he knew what was going on. I felt bad for the guy – it wasn't so long ago that I was having stuff chucked at me.

We ran to catch up with him.

'New bag, Rex?' I said, nodding at his fancy backpack. It was a big improvement on his old one that was covered in strange stains.

'Yeah,' he said, staring at his shoes.

'It's the only thing he owns that he didn't get out

of the charity shop,' Jason said, laughing with the others.

'Shut up, Jason,' I shouted. 'Or I'll set Jess on you.'

'I'm not scared of you or your freak girlfriend,' Jason said. But he turned to the others. 'Come on, let's go and play on Ronnie's Xbox. I'm not getting a new one till Saturday.'

They walked off in the opposite direction.

'Jess isn't my girlfriend, by the way,' I said to Rex.

'Thank goodness,' said Jess.

'She's actually shipped with Darth Daver. You know, the tallest boy in the school with the long hair. He's also my best mate, FYI.'

Rex said nothing. It was pretty awkward – the walk to the sanctuary seemed to take a lot longer than it had the day before.

When we reached the sanctuary and had changed into our overalls, Rex led us through the rooms. As we walked, I noticed a door that had a PRIVATE sign on it.

'Is that the office?' I said.

'Yes,' said Rex.

'Are you allowed in there?'

'No.'

'Have you ever sneaked in?' I asked.

'No,' Rex grunted.

He was lying. Jess sniffed and looked at me and I nodded. Things at this animal sanctuary were getting more and more interesting.

The sanctuary felt different today. There was an atmosphere: the animals were quiet and on edge.

For the first ten minutes, stuff went on pretty much as it had the day before. We filled the food bowls – well, Jess filled most of them. I didn't mind doing the ones with mushy fruit and vegetables but I couldn't deal with the blood and entrails.

'Anyone would think you were the vegetarian,' Jess said, sighing at me.

'The stuff I eat doesn't have obvious body parts mixed in with it,' I said. 'If you don't really think about it, you can kid yourself that a chicken burger is made of sugar and Weetabix. There's no pretending with this goo. You can see the hearts and eyeballs.'

We'd just finished lining the bowls up on the counter when we heard a phone ring somewhere in the building. Two minutes later, Mrs Rex's mum rushed into the room, doing another one of her special whistles. It was higher and louder than the one we heard the day before, and it kind of curled upwards. As soon as Rex heard it, he rushed to grab a bag of supplies.

'What is it?' Jess said.

'Emergency callout,' said Rex. 'Medium-sized sheep with suspected broken leg and bleeding wound.'

He got all that from a whistle?

'I hope they can be trusted,' Rex's mum said, looking at us. 'Let's go. Rex: to heel!'

'Just do the same as you did yesterday,' Rex said, then trotted after his mum. The door banged as they left the building.

I turned to Jess. 'I know exactly where we should go first.'

'Let me guess…'

'Follow me!'

I picked up a bowl of meaty chunks and ran outside to enclosure 17.

'Mr Prickles?' I called, and I was just about to call again when his little black nose poked out of the doorway of his house, almost like he'd been waiting for me. I was so happy to see his furry face. I climbed over the fence into his enclosure and put his food on the floor. I was almost afraid to look at Jess because I thought she'd make fun of me – I could feel my cheeks getting hot. But she didn't say anything, just came and sat next to me on the log. Mr Prickles ignored his food bowl and instead snuffled his way towards me. When he reached my foot, he gently butted his head against my ankle so I laid my hand on the floor and he climbed into it.

'Hey there, mate. How are you doing today?' I said, as I lifted him close to my face. He licked my nose. 'This is my friend, Jess. You can talk to her – she'll understand you.'

Mr Prickles looked at Jess and she started to twitch away. It was painful waiting to hear what he'd said.

When Jess stopped jerking around, she looked at me and smiled.

'What?' I said. 'What did he say? Does he like me? What's his real name?'

'He's never had a name before,' she said. 'But he really likes Mr Prickles because you chose it for him, so he's going to keep it.'

I thought my heart would burst.

'He's been at the sanctuary for a long time. He can't go back into the wild because of his bad eye and nose, so he has to stay here forever. He's a bit lonely, so he's really happy that he has a friend now.'

I put Mr Prickles on to my shoulder and he cuddled into me. His spikes scratched a bit, but I didn't care.

'Thanks, Mr Prickles,' I said. 'Besties for life?' I held my knuckles up to him. He sniffed them, then curled up his tiny paw, so I bumped it against mine.

'Mr Prickles,' I said. 'Do you know anything about The Rattler?'

Mr Prickles squeaked, curled up into a ball and plopped off my shoulder into my lap, narrowly missing my boy bits, which was a relief because that would really hurt.

'I know you're scared,' I said. 'But if you can be brave and tell Jess everything you know, we might be able to help.'

He unfurled himself slightly so we could see his face amongst the prickles. Then Jess started to twitch. For the first time ever, it bothered me that she could understand an animal and I couldn't. I know Mr Prickles and me had our own way of communicating, but I would have loved to hear what he had to say.

'And do you know anything about animals acting strangely in the outside world?' Jess said, then spasmed again before thanking Mr Prickles for his help.

'So?' I said, trying not to make it obvious how annoyed I was that Jess knew what *my* hedgehog had said.

'OK,' said Jess, tickling Mr Prickles under his snout. 'The Rattler comes at night, dressed in dark colours with a hood pulled low over his face. The animals call him The Rattler because he carries a bunch of keys that he can use to open any of the doors and cages in the sanctuary. He shakes them as he moves around in the dark.'

'So far, so creepy,' I said.

'He doesn't come every night, just once every couple of weeks. They never know exactly when he's going to come, but they dread it. If weeks have passed without him coming, they start to get scared because they know he'll be back soon.'

'Because they don't like the rattling?' It seemed a bit of an over-reaction.

'Because every time he comes, he takes one of them. They never know who it will be, but it's a different type of animal each time. He chooses someone to take, abducts them from their enclosure and leaves.'

'And what happens then?' I asked, feeling sick.

'They don't know,' said Jess. 'The Rattler comes back a few weeks later to take another animal, but the animals who get taken never return. Nobody sees or hears from them ever again. He came last night – that's why they're all so quiet today. He took a tortoise called Sir Blimmo.'

'Son of a biscuit.' I could understand why they were all so terrified. Imagine some creepy stranger coming into your house at night, stealing you out of your bed and taking you who knows where.

'Sir Blimmo was the oldest animal here. He'd survived three dog attacks, a runaway lawnmower, and a firework incident. He seemed indestructible. The animals are all in shock.'

'Sorry, Mr Prickles,' I said, 'Sir Blimmo sounds like a boss.' I pulled a handful of treats that I'd brought with me out of my pocket and fed them to Mr Prickles.

'What are they?' Jess said.

'Mealworms. Apparently they're like candy for hedgehogs.'

'Alex Sparrow, have you been researching hedgehogs? On your own? Just because you want to?' Jess's face was doing something weird that was like a cross between shock and laughter.

'I wanted to do something to make him happy,' I said.

'You're getting too close to that hedgehog,' Rex's voice floated through the shrubs, followed by Rex's face and Rex's body. It made me jump out of my skin. I swear he's part chameleon. 'He's a wild animal. Things happen to animals. You need to stay detached.'

'That seems a bit harsh, Rex,' I said. 'After all, the animals are perfectly safe here, aren't they?'

'Yeah,' he said. *Lie.*

'Do you have the medium-sized sheep?' I said, as innocently as possible.

'Fake callout,' he said. 'I'm going to feed the reptiles.'

'We need more time alone, so we can find out what's going on,' Jess whispered to me as soon as he'd walked off.

'Fear not, Jessticles. I have an amazing plan.'

# 6

## The Great Esssssssscape

I crept towards the reptile room while Jess was busy outside. I knew she'd hate my plan, but I was going to do it anyway, and it would be better if I could do it without her shouting at me. The reptile room was the smallest room in the sanctuary. It had a sliding door that was kept closed all the time, and inside it was darkish and warm. Rex had shown Jess and me inside on the first day but told us we weren't allowed to go in there by ourselves. Ever. Of course, that was basically an invitation to peep in whenever I had an opportunity, so I'd been in a couple of times, just for a minute.

I hid outside the door and waited. A few minutes later, the door slid open, and Rex walked out, carrying some empty feeding containers. His hands were full, so he used his elbow to slide the door shut again behind him. I held my breath as he walked past, half convinced that he was going to sniff me out. But he didn't. He left the room and moved towards the kitchen. 'Ha!' I thought. 'Now, who's the master of camouflagery?' I tiptoed to the reptile room door, slid it open and slipped inside.

I'm not going to lie, the reptile room was a bit spooky – some of the creatures in there looked like total bad-As. I located the tank I was looking for and carefully approached. Inside was a corn snake. It was only as wide as a cucumber but it must have been about three metres long. It was quite cool looking – all orange with red markings and gleaming black and orange eyes.

'Hey,' I said. 'Totes sorry to disturb, but I have a proposition for you.'

The snake's tail shifted slightly, but other than that it remained still.

'Listen. I know you can understand me and I know you want to escape this place, so I was hoping we could do each other a favour.'

The snake lifted his head and looked at me, his tongue flickering.

'So I have your attention,' I said. 'Here's the offer: I'm going to open your tank and open the door and you can flee to freedom. In return, I need you to promise not to eat any of the animals in the sanctuary...' I hard-eyed him. 'None of them. Not even a tiny snack. What you do outside here is your business, although it would be great if you could stick to rummaging through bins for half-eaten McDonalds.'

He started to uncoil himself.

'Is that a promise?' I asked. 'Tap your tail against the glass if you agree.'

The corn snake writhed around in his tank, sliding his whole body against the glass wall. I had to admit, he was an impressive guy. The way he moved was like nothing I'd ever seen before.

'Cool – we have a deal,' I said. 'And there's one more thing. You have to make sure that Rex's mum sees you before you leave the sanctuary. I know it's a lot to ask, when you could just be wriggling out into the great wide world, but it's really important and I would totally appreciate it. I know there's something bad going down here – something to do with The Rattler. I'm trying to put a stop to it and this is all part of the plan. So if you're at all interested in helping your fellow animals, please do this for me.'

He dipped his head. I think he understood but once again I wished for a bit of Jess's power so that I could know for sure. If Jess was there she would ask if he agreed, but he could still lie about it. If we had a super-mega-combo of mine and Jess's powers, we could understand him and know if he was telling the truth. But for now, I just had to trust him.

I took a deep breath and opened the lid of his tank, then I left the room, sliding the door behind me so that it was almost shut, but leaving a gap big enough for the snake to squeeze through. I ran back out to the garden, whizzed by enclosure 17 and then found Jess.

'Are we good to go?' Jess said.

I gave her my smuggest smile and a thumbs-up.

'Alex,' Jess said, looking down at my bottom area. 'Why are you walking funny? And what's that in your pocket?'

'Nothing!'

'It's definitely not nothing. It's moving.'

Mr Prickles popped his little head out.

'Alex!' Jess said. 'You have to put him back – we'll get into so much trouble!'

'Chill out, Jessticles. I will, I promise. After.'

'After what?'

Right on schedule, a sequence of high-pitched whistles shrieked through the building like a fire alarm. I heard a crash in the kitchen, and Rex came running outside.

'What is it?' Jess said.

'Code Red,' Rex shouted, as though that explained everything.

Rex's mum bowled across the garden to him. She was carrying a sack and a long stick with a loop at the end of it. 'I just checked, Rex – its tank and the reptile room door were open. How could you forget your training like that?'

Rex looked gutted and, yeah, I did feel a bit guilty.

'I don't know, Mum. I swear I shut them. I thought I did, anyway, but I was carrying all the feeding equipment.'

'Bad boy,' Rex's mum said. 'Looks like you need some time back in bootcamp.'

Rex hung his head. 'I'll find it, Mum – we'll get it back.'

Jess raised an eyebrow at me.

'It came to the office and bashed the door,' Rex's mum said. 'If I didn't know better, I'd swear it was laughing at me.'

Jess couldn't take it any longer. 'Has something escaped?' she called over to Rex and his mum.

'Code Red,' said Rex. 'The five-foot corn snake.'

Jess gasped in horror, which worked really well as part of the plan. Obviously it was directed at me, but nobody else knew that.

'The escapee will be found and returned to custody,' Rex's mum said. 'You two continue with your work, and Rex and I will commence search and rescue.'

'OMG!' I said, pointing at the back of the garden. 'I think I just saw something orange going over the wall!' A nasty stink enveloped my nostrils and Jess gave me another one of her looks.

'Rex! To heel!' Mrs Rex whistled and they ran off.

Jess turned to me. 'What did you do, Alex?'

'Made a deal with a corn snake.'

'You helped it escape?' I thought she'd be impressed but she actually looked horrified. 'Alex, that's so dangerous.'

'Don't worry,' I said. 'Mr Prickles is safe.'

'What about the other animals?' she said.

'We spoke about it and he promised he wouldn't eat anyone in the sanctuary. I wouldn't have let him out without checking that first. Duh.'

'How do you know he promised? You can't understand animals.'

'I had to take a chance, Jessticles. Sometimes in life, you just have to YOLO it.'

'Alex, you can be so irresponsible.'

'You were fine when Harry Potter did it,' I said.

'Alex, that's a story – this is real life!'

We were wasting precious time.

'It's done now, Jess, so we can either stand here arguing about it or we can use the time to try to save the poor animals in this place from the real danger. Do the animals know who The Rattler is?'

Jess juddered away with a bunch of rabbits. 'They don't. They never get a good look at him but these rabbits say he smells different from the other people who come here.'

'Are you sure it's not Rex?' I asked a rabbit

called Piper. 'Or Mrs Rex's mum? She's quite scary.'

'She's quite sure it's not anyone who works here,' Jess said.

'And what about the stuff going on outside the sanctuary? Do they know anything about that?'

'They've been here a while so they don't know. They said the best thing to do would be to ask an animal who's just been brought in. They might know.'

'Do you really think Rex and his mum don't have anything to do with The Rattler?' I said to Jess. 'They're so weird.'

'Alex, you should know better than anyone that being weird doesn't make you evil.'

'I suppose that's true,' I said. 'You're not evil, after all. But how can this be going on without them knowing? Surely they'd notice the animals going missing. It doesn't make sense.'

Jess looked at me. 'Office first?'

'Affirmative.'

We raced through the building to the door marked PRIVATE.

'Would you like to do the honours, Jess?' I said, and she pushed the door open.

I don't know what I was expecting from this top-secret, nobody's-allowed-in room but, I have to say, I was disappointed. It was tiny – more like a big cupboard than an actual room – and all it had in it was a desk, a chair and a couple of shelves. Everything was in a total mess and covered with dust. There was no computer, just a rubbish-looking television and one of those house phones that my mum insists on having even though no one interesting calls on it because everyone has a mobile. The shelves were stacked with books about animals and first aid, and the desk was covered in tea stains and chocolate wrappers.

'It looks like Rex's mum just sits in here stuffing her face and watching TV while we do all the work,' I said. 'No wonder she won't let us in.'

'There must be something here,' said Jess. 'Some files or something. Rex said they kept records.'

I opened the desk drawer. Inside was a faded, dirty A4-sized notebook.

'Aha!' I pulled it out and opened it.

It was a list of enclosure numbers with the animals living in each written next to them. There was basic information about each animal – breed, sex, approximate age and any injuries or illnesses it had.

'This is it!' I said. 'What are we looking for exactly?'

'Something about what happens to the animals when they disappear. There must be a note of what happens to them.'

I turned the pages. 'Oh, look!'

'What is it? What have you found?' Jess peered over my shoulder.

'Enclosure 17,' I read. 'Hedgehog, male, approximately three years old, blind in right eye. It's Mr Prickles' stats!'

Mr Prickles snuffled in my pocket when he heard his name.

'Give it here,' Jess huffed. She flicked through the pages. 'Most of the animals have been here a while, but some of them have a line through them. Look: this one says rehomed, this one deceased, this one escaped.'

'So what we need to know is if these are the creatures that were taken by The Rattler,' I said.

'And if they are, why are they being marked down as dead or rehomed?'

'We need copies,' I said. 'Do you think there's a photocopier here?'

'Use your phone.'

I pulled my phone out of my pocket and activated Siri. 'Siri. Where can I find a photocopying shop in my local area?'

'Hello Mr Stark,' Siri answered. 'I have found no matches for phone to coffee and shark in your local area.'

'For God's sake, Alex,' Jess said, snatching my phone out of my hand.

'Try to speak really clearly,' I said. 'Siri is slightly deaf.'

Jess pressed the screen a few times and gave the phone back to me with the camera on.

'You want to do a selfie? I'm not sure it's really the time, but I'm always up for a selfie. Best agent faces on three...'

'Take photos of the records, Alex.' Jess sighed so hard.

'That's actually a really good idea, Jessticles,' I said. 'Or should I call you The Jerky Genius?' I took a bunch of pictures on my phone camera.

'OK,' Jess said. 'Now we can find out who the most recent addition to the sanctuary was and ask them about the animal incidents.'

I turned to the last entry in the book. 'It's the deer in critical care. Excellent – another place we've been forbidden from visiting. I do like to get my money's worth out of a sub-mission.'

'What exactly is a sub-mission?'

'It's a mission within a mission, obviously. And this one is called Operation Rattle Snake. You know, because of The Rattler, and the corn snake?'

'Yeah, I get it.'

'Alex and Jess be using their ability to infiltrate a top-secret facility...'

'I wish you'd stop trying to rap.'

'Off to critical care!' I shoved the notebook back in the drawer. 'Make sure you close the door, Jess,' I said. 'We don't want to end up in trouble like that careless Rex.'

'But Rex didn't do anything. You were the one who opened the doors.'

'Depends how you look at it.'

I checked Mr Prickles was alright in my pocket and then I started jogging towards the garden.

'No. No, it doesn't.' I could hear Jess huffing even though she was quite a way behind me.

I stopped outside the critical-care unit. 'So this is a deer, right?' I said to Jess. 'Like a cute Bambi thing.'

'Sure,' she said. 'All wild animals are based on cartoon characters.'

I lifted the latch and opened the door. It was nicer inside than I'd expected – separated into different-sized pens and areas, dim but not dark and with a nice woody smell. All of the enclosures were empty, so it was quiet and calm.

'I could chill in here,' I said.

'Over there.' Jess pointed to a large fenced-off area in the far corner. 'And go carefully, remember she's badly hurt. We don't want to upset her.'

Lying on the floor on a pile of straw was the deer. She was much bigger than I'd thought and her fur was a plain brownish-red. She had one leg in a plaster cast thing, and large cuts all over her face and body that were mostly healed but still looked sore. She looked up at us and made a weird squeaky growl noise.

'I'll talk to her first,' I said. 'I'm good with animals now.'

Jess raised an eyebrow but didn't try to stop me.

I stepped forward. 'Hey. I'm Agent Alex – you might have heard of me. I recently saved my school from an evil teacher. And this is Jess. She helped a bit, too.'

The deer just stared.

'So, we were hoping you'd be able to answer a few questions about some incidents that have taken place over the last few weeks: howling foxes and ninja squirrels, that sort of thing. Is that cool?'

The deer parted her lips – do deers have lips? – showing her front teeth, and then she made this noise that started as a squeaky growl and grew into a squeaky roar.

I stepped back. 'I'm not sure what that was, Jess, but I think she's mad.'

'I would have told you that, but I thought you had it under control because, you know, you're good with animals now.'

'I'm better with cartoon deers than actual ones,' I said. 'Over to you.'

'How are you feeling?' Jess walked over to the enclosure. 'I'm sorry about your accident.'

The deer squowled again and Jess started to twitch.

'That's awful,' Jess said to the deer. 'But please understand that we aren't all like that. We want to help.'

The deer butted her head upwards and

screeched. If she could have stood up, I'm pretty sure she would have attacked us.

'I think she wants to hurt us,' I whispered. 'Lucky she hasn't got those deer horns.'

'You mean antlers, Alex. Antlers. And she's female.'

'No need to be sexist, Jessticles. I'm sure girl deers can impale people with their deer horns, too.'

'We should go,' Jess said, backing towards the door.

'Defos.'

We opened the door and stepped back into the garden, which seemed like an extra wonderful place now that we'd been in critical care with a raging deer. Jess followed me to enclosure 17, where I settled Mr Prickles back into his house.

'I was wrong, Jess,' I said.

'About the deer and the antlers? Of course you were.'

'No, I mean I was wrong when I said I could chill in there. I could not chill in there. The deer stuff I was technically right about.'

'Yeah, things aren't so chill right now.'

'What did you find out? Did the deer tell you anything?'

'She wouldn't say much – she's too angry.'

'With who?'

'With humans.'

'Because she was in an accident with a car?'

'That's the thing,' Jess said. 'It wasn't an accident. She was standing in the road, trying to stop a van from passing. A van that was carrying stolen animals.'

I gasped.

'The driver deliberately ran into her. She was hit on purpose.'

'No wonder she's annoyed,' I said. 'Did she say anything else?'

'Just one more thing, but she kept repeating it over and over again.'

'What?'

'The Storm.'

# 7

## Secret Codes and
## Broken Fences

The next day was Saturday, and me and Jess were walking to the sanctuary.

'I'm just going to text my homies,' I said.

'You mean your mum?'

I chose to ignore her. I might only be texting my mum, but the joy of texting on my new phone was so immense that I could have been texting Miss Smilie in jail and it wouldn't have mattered. In fact, that would be sick. 'Hey Ms S Life is gr8 now ur gone. Hope jail $uck$. Agent A. xoxo.' I pulled my phone out of my pocket and started tapping away. I liked to have the keyboard clicks on because it really annoyed Jess. I got busy with my fingers to the beautiful sound of Jess tutting next to me, but I couldn't escape the feeling that we were being watched. I looked behind us but there was nobody there.

'What's wrong?' Jess said.

'I'm not sure,' I said. 'My agent sense is tingling.'

'You said that a couple of days ago and then it turned out you just needed to sneeze.'

'Yeah,' I said. 'It's probably nothing.'

We turned into Cherry Tree Lane to see a commotion on the pavement outside our school. There was a police car and an ambulance parked up with their blue lights flashing and a news crew setting up cameras.

'You see,' I said, tapping my nose. 'Agent sense. Never fails. Although I need to think of a better name than agent sense. It only works for Spider-Man because of the 's'es. Agent anticipation? Nah, that's rubbish.'

'Focus, Alex,' Jess said, running towards the scene. I put my phone in my pocket and followed.

There was a lady sitting at the open back of the ambulance with a paramedic holding a cloth to a cut on her head. She was talking to a policeman who was writing things down in a notebook.

'What happened?' Jess asked a nosy bystander.

'One of them squirrel muggings,' the man said. 'Cut her head and smashed her brand new iPhone. Poor love. What's the world coming to, eh?'

The news crew was standing in front of the taped-off area, obviously filming live.

'Look, there's Taran!' Jess said, pointing at a dashing-looking figure standing close to the news reporter. 'Are you thinking what I'm thinking?'

'That we should photobomb the news report?' I said, thinking how cool it would be to be on the news again.

'Or something less immature,' said Jess. 'I was thinking he must be the animal expert they keep talking to about these incidents. Maybe we should try to spend some time with him and see what we can learn.'

'Yeah, that's why you want to spend time with him.'

'What's that supposed to mean?'

'It means you've obviously got a giant crush on him.'

'Why would you think something so stupid?' Jess's face was bright pink.

'You wouldn't twitch in front of him, you ignored the fact that he told you a lie and you practically dribbled on his shoes,' I said. 'He could be The Rattler for all we know.'

'He can't be The Rattler, Alex. Your flipping hedgehog told us it isn't anyone who works at the sanctuary.'

She had me there.

'Well, if you don't have a crush, you won't mind going up to Taran right now and talking to Meena.'

'I hate you sometimes, Alex!'

Jess stomped past me, knocking me backwards into one of the big cherry trees. To be fair, I may have exaggerated the fall a little bit.

'Oh gosh, I'm so sorry,' she said, turning back to help me up. 'I didn't mean to hurt you.'

'It's ok, Jess. It's mostly my pride.'

'Wait, what's that behind you?'

'There can't be anything behind me, Jess, or my agent alert would have tingled.' Agent alert was better.

'Look, Alex – I don't remember seeing this before.'

I turned to see what she was looking at. There was something scratched into the bark of the tree trunk – words written in such messed-up, scrawly writing that it was hard to make them out at first. It was weird. People don't usually take the time to scratch rude words into trees. If you got caught you'd be in loads of trouble, and there's no point when you can just post whatever you like anonymously on the internet.

'I think it's a code,' I said. 'Look, there's a cross – maybe that represents Jesus or something, and then it says "HISTORY SCREAMING".'

'Are you sure that's what it says?' said Jess. 'It doesn't make any sense.' She rubbed over the letters with her fingers.

'Careful, Jessticles, don't touch it – it might be poisoned. I don't need a dead sidekick on my hands. And also, of course it doesn't make sense. It's a secret code.'

'Why would it be poisoned?' Jess sighed.

'Did you not hear me say "secret code"? There's something sinister about it.'

'You think that about everything.'

'Not *everything*,' I said. 'But you've got to admit, it's suspicious.'

A rustle in the branches above us made us both look up.

'Maybe we shouldn't stand here,' Jess said. 'Let's go say hi to Taran. It would be rude not to.'

We walked over to the film crew. The reporter was just wrapping up the interview and thanking Taran, who spotted us a moment later.

'Hi, Jess and Alex,' he said. 'How's it going?'

'Brilliant, thanks, Taran,' Jess beamed. 'Hello, Meena.' She patted Meena on the head.

'Are you enjoying working at the sanctuary?' Taran said. 'I know Mrs Fernandes can take a bit of getting used to.'

'Who's Mrs Fernandes?' I said.

'Rex's mum, you idiot,' Jess glared at me. She turned to Taran. 'I'm absolutely loving it – I'm so grateful for the opportunity. But we wanted to ask you what you think is happening with these animal attacks. We'd really value your expert opinion.'

Jeez – why was Jess talking like an alien?

'That's a very good question, Jess, and the most truthful answer is that nobody is sure. There are lots of theories circulating...' (Jess was nodding thoughtfully, and for once I got to roll my eyes at her) '...some people think it's connected to climate change, some that the destruction of the squirrels' natural habitat is making them behave more aggressively...'

He went on like that for ages. It was all very boring and not useful to our mission at all, but Jess kept asking more questions and sucking it all up. Of course, I kept my ear on high alert, but it didn't make a peep.

I got my phone out and checked my text messages, WhatsApp, voicemails and emails to pass the time. I got the feeling that my input wasn't needed in the conversation anyway.

'Sorry to interrupt,' I said finally, 'but it's 12:55.'

'Oh gosh, we have to go,' Jess said. 'Thank you so much for taking the time to talk to us.'

'Anytime. Always happy to help a fellow animal lover. Hopefully bump into you again soon.'

Meena whined. I'm pretty sure she felt the same way I did about this whole boring and uncomfortable situation. I gave her a solidarity smile.

'Hopefully.' Jess did this weird giggly thing.

'What's funny?' I said.

'Shut up, Alex. Bye Taran, bye Meena.' She waved and we finally got to leave.

'Why do you have to be such a jerk, Alex?' Jess had the serious hump.

'It's another one of my many skills.'

When we reached the sanctuary, we were greeted by a miserable-looking Rex.

'Did you find the snake?' Jess asked them, looking genuinely concerned.

Rex shook his head. 'No, but there's a loose section in the back fence. It looks like something's been trying to force its way out.'

'Or trying to find a way in.' Rex's mum appeared in the doorway. 'I'm locking up early today so that Rex and I can secure the sanctuary. Get on with your jobs. Make it quick.'

As soon as I could, I dragged Jess over to enclosure 17.

'Did you break the fence, Alex?' Jess said, as I picked Mr Prickles up for a snuggle. 'Another stupidly risky part of your escaping snake plan?'

'I didn't touch the fence! A security breach like that would mean anything could get into the sanctuary. I want Mr Prickles to be safe. And I don't want The Rattler to get him. In fact, I'm going to sneak him out today.' I couldn't stand the thought of leaving him there.

'You can't – we'll lose our jobs and we need to find out what's going on here.'

'But I can't bear to think about something awful happening to him.' I looked down at his adorable face.

'I know you're worried about him, but he's been here for years and he's never been taken. I'm sure he's quite safe.'

'But Jess…' I said, feeling like I might cry. I cuddled Mr Prickles into my chest.

Jess twitched for a few seconds. 'Mr Prickles says he wants to stay. He doesn't want us to lose our jobs because then nobody will ever stop The Rattler.'

'Mr Prickles, you are a brave little dude,' I said and I walked him back to his enclosure.

As soon as I knew Jess was too far away to hear, I whispered, 'When all this is over, I'll find a way for us to be together. I promise.' Then I set him down at the front of his house. 'Stay safe.'

# 8

## A Costly Breakthrough

Jess had decided to come over to my house after our shift so we could talk about everything we'd found out.

As we walked up Cherry Tree Lane past school – which I always like doing on Saturdays because you get to have that epic feeling of not having to go in – I saw a familiar person approaching, half dragging something on a lead behind him.

'Oh man, it's Jason,' I said. 'Looks like he got a

new dog. Shall we cross the road so we don't have to listen to the abuse he will no doubt shout at us?'

Jess laughed. 'Do you remember when you were all, "I want to be best friends with Jason, he's so awesome"?'

'That was ages ago, Jess.'

'By which you mean about four weeks.'

'Whatever. Let's cross.'

'No way. I'm not going out of my way to get out of his way. If we cross it will look like we're scared of him.'

So we carried on towards him. His new dog was really small. Like Mr Prickles would beat it in a fight small. It had bulgy eyes and tufty hair and obviously didn't like Jason very much because it kept trying to run away.

'Scuzzo! Freak girl!' Jason said when he saw us. 'Been working at the kennels with Dog Boy? You must smell even worse than usual.'

'Jason,' I said. 'Always a pleasure.'

'Everyone knows about your stinky job and that you're hanging around with Rex. I bet it was all three of you who set my Xbox on fire.'

Jason's dog started jumping and barking.

'Shut up, Fleur!' he shouted, yanking at her

lead. 'What the hell is wrong with your freak girlfriend, Scuzzo? You should really take her to a vet.'

Jess was jerking around quite violently and stuttering out a few words here and there. I always like to try to guess what her conversations are about from the way she twitches. I guessed that this wasn't a very friendly chat. Jason stomped off, pulling Fleur, who seemed surprisingly strong for such a tiny dog.

'What was that about?' I asked Jess.

'She was laughing about the Xbox,' Jess said, 'so I asked her why. She said she was the one who started the fire. She weed on the Xbox on purpose.'

'I know Jason's a total jerk, but was there a specific reason?'

'I asked her that, too, and do you know what she said?'

'Because she was mad that she couldn't make platinum on *Overwatch* and it was her version of a rage-quit?' It was the only justification I could think of.

'Funnily enough, no,' said Jess. 'She just laughed again and said, "The storm is coming."'

'This is all very confusing.'

We were sitting at the breakfast bar, drinking milkshake. Well, I was drinking milkshake and Jess was drinking some gross-tasting liquid made out of coconut and almonds.

'I feel like we need to make a list. Shall we make a list?'

'What kind of list?'

'A list of the things we know and the things we don't know. There are still some blank pages in our old mission log.'

'But what if it falls into the wrong hands?' Jess wiggled her eyebrows at me in an extremely annoying way, but she had a point.

'As soon as we're done, you'll have to eat it,' I said.

'I'm not eating a homework diary.'

'Why not? It's paper. Paper comes from trees. You're a vegan so trees are one of your five main food groups.'

'Shall we get started?' Jess sighed.

'We need two columns. One for the sanctuary and one for the other incidents.'

'I'm doing the writing then, am I?'

'Item one for the sanctuary: The Rattler. He

comes at night and takes an animal each time. Identity unknown.'

'Item two,' Jess said, scribbling away. 'The log book. Someone is recording the animals as being rehomed or dead. We need get a list of the animals who've disappeared and see if it matches the log.'

'And we need to find out who's been updating the log,' I said.

'Mrs Fernandes seems the most likely person,' said Jess. 'And she's very secretive about the office.'

'But I know that Rex has snuck in there, and that he's been lying about other stuff.'

'Right. I think that's everything.'

'Not quite...' I side-eyed Jess. 'We know Taran hasn't been completely honest with us.'

'That was probably one of those nothing lies. Like saying you're fine when someone asks how you are, when you're really feeling like you want to punch your friend Alex in the face.'

I pulled my stool away a little. 'But we don't know that for sure. I feel like we shouldn't ignore it.'

'The animals said that The Rattler isn't anyone who works there.'

'But that doesn't mean Rex, his mum and Taran aren't involved in what's going on. They might know something.'

Jess glared at me. 'Let's start the animal-incident column. Item one: the squirrel attacks. They seem to be going after people's phones. Item two: the howling foxes.'

'Item three: Jason's dog blowing up his Xbox.'

I thought for a moment while Jess finished writing. 'Then there's the angry deer – she needs to go in both columns. She was grievously injured in a deliberate hit and run attack when she tried to intercept…'

'…a van containing stolen animals.' Jess looked at me.

'Are you thinking what I'm thinking, my trusty sidekick?' I said.

'The stolen animals,' Jess said. 'Could some of the missing animals from the sanctuary have been in that van?'

I jumped off my stool, knocking it over in the process, much to Bob's annoyance. I could see him flapping about in the corner of my eye. 'The two things *are* connected!'

'But how?'

'I don't know exactly, but I think it has something to do with what Jason's dog said, and the deer. And do you remember the code on the tree?'

'The one you thought said "HISTORY SCREAMING" with a cross next to it?'

'I don't remember saying that at all, Jessticles. But, moving quickly on, if you write it down, look...'

I grabbed the list from Jess and scribbled down the markings we'd seen on the tree.

'You know, I think you've got something,' said Jess, peering at the paper. 'I think it says, The Storm Is Coming. But what does it mean? An actual storm? Some kind of metaphor?' She wrote it in capital letters across the bottom of the page. Then she started to twitch. 'Bob has something to say that we might find useful.'

'What does he want now?' I sighed. 'And how much money and-slash-or time is it going to take?'

'Just a sec – he has a list,' Jess said, and she jerked around for a minute. 'OK. Bob and Elle have decided that the only way they can move in together without one of them feeling upset is by getting a completely new place that they can make their own as a couple.'

'Right – a new tank. Sounds expensive.'

'However, before they select their new home, they want to ensure they are fully informed and prepared…'

'Huh?'

'They want to peruse a catalogue of potential homes and a wide selection of interior-design magazines.'

'How are they going to turn the pages?' I said.

'We have to peruse with them,' said Jess.

'Of course we do.'

'Apparently this is all essential if they are to have a future of domestic bliss.'

I peered into Bob's tank. 'This had better be good, Agent Bob.'

Jess twitched away.

'Well?' I said.

'He said we're looking at things the wrong way – the phrase we keep hearing isn't "A Storm Is Coming", it's "The Storm Is Coming."'

'So what? Is there a difference?'

'Bob says that "A Storm" suggests an actual storm or something that happens regularly. "The

Storm" suggests there is only one. He thinks "The Storm" could be a person.'

'Son of a biscuit!' I said. 'The Storm and The Rattler! Finally some proper bad-guy secret identities. This case is getting more exciting by the minute.'

'And talking of excitement,' Jess said, pulling her coat on. 'We'd better get to the shops for those magazines.'

# 9

## I Have a Seriously Bad Day

The next day we got a message from Rex telling us the animal sanctuary was still on lockdown while they looked for the missing snake.

'How frustrating,' Jess said. 'I was hoping we could get that list of missing animals today. I'm sure Mr Prickles would have helped us with it.'

'He would have. And now we don't get to see him until after school tomorrow. That's ages.'

'Ask your mum if we can go out for a walk – we can have a look around.'

'Ooh – we can hunt for animals doing things they shouldn't be!' It was probably the only thing that could have cheered me up. 'Agent A is back on the case, wreaking havoc on the streets like there's no time to waste.'

'Please stop.'

'Sorry, Jessticles. I can't hear you over the dull hum of boringness that's radiating out of you.'

'Just get your coat on.'

'I'm too bad-A for a coat.'

'When you're cold you whimper like a baby.'

'Because it hurts, Jess. It literally physically hurts.' I hated when Jess was right.

A minute later, with my hat pulled low and my coat done up to the top, we left my house and started walking towards the park. We figured we were more likely to come across animals there than on the streets.

We had to cross the road I live on, which is always quite busy with cars. I looked both ways about ten times before I stepped out because I knew my mum would be watching from the window and if she saw me mucking about, she'd never let me out of the house on my own again. We were halfway across when it was like the ground gave way beneath me, and I found myself stacking it.

'What the heck?' I said, as my elbow scraped across the tarmac and everything moved in slow motion.

'Alex!' Jess shouted, reaching out to grab me.

A car screeched to a stop centimetres away from where I was lying on the floor.

I heard a scream and Mum came sprinting out into the road. 'Alex! Are you OK?'

I looked down at the ground to see a large hole beneath where the tarmac had crumbled away. It must have been a metre deep.

'I'm fine, Mum,' I said, which was a massive lie because my elbow stung like half my skin had been peeled off, and my heart was racing. An eggy stench seeped into the air.

The driver got out of the car to see if I was alright, and a crowd of neighbours gathered round to make a fuss. Normally I'd like the attention, but I just wanted to get on with our mission.

'It's lucky you found that sinkhole,' the car driver said, as though I'd been especially clever to fall over in the middle of the road. 'If I'd driven over it, I could have had a nasty accident.'

'You can give me a reward if you like,' I said, while Mum checked me over and started ranting about calling the council and the police and the fire brigade.

The car driver laughed like I was joking.

A whole queue of cars had built up, and everyone was leaning out of their windows to see what was going on.

'We need to get this road closed off!' my next-door neighbour said. 'Honestly, I don't know what the world is coming to. First Colin and now this.'

I didn't really see how his missing cat and the hole in the road were connected but it seemed rude to say so.

'Can I go, Mum?' I said. 'I'm honestly alright.'

'If you're sure, my love,' she said. 'But please text me when you get to the park so I know you're OK.'

'Don't worry, Mrs Sparrow,' said Jess, 'I'll look after him.'

We crossed the road, leaving chaos behind us and walked towards the park. I rolled up my sleeve to inspect my arm injury.

'That was weird,' Jess said. 'It looked like something had dug a hole under the road. You're surprisingly OK about that enormous scrape on your arm.'

'I am not OK, Jess,' I said. 'It hurts so bad, I think I might cry. But if I told my mum she would have made me go home.'

'Let's focus on the mission, then. I know I'll regret saying this, but talk me through your thoughts.'

'OK. I think The Rattler and The Storm are super-villain teammates whose sole purpose in life is to destroy the world as we know it. They've trained animals to carry out their orders and their plan is to take out our infrastructure. So they've trained the squirrels to destroy our phones, and the foxes to make sure we don't sleep.'

'And this super-villain team is responsible for the hole in the road, too, are they?'

'They probably trained the moles or the badgers to do their evil bidding.'

'It's an interesting theory,' Jess said, which meant she was trying to be nice to me because I was close to death. Really she thought my theory was stupid. 'But we don't have any evidence to suggest that the badgers and moles have turned against us.'

'Of course the badgers are against us,' I said. 'We culled them.'

'I actually wrote to the Prime Minister about that.'

'Of course you did.'

'But that doesn't mean they made the hole in the road.'

'Do you know what else I've noticed?' We were walking up the hill to the park.

'I'm sure you're going to tell me.'

'Between my house and here, I've seen four different posters on lampposts for missing pets: three cats and a dog.'

Jess stopped walking suddenly. 'You're actually right.'

'I'm going to pretend you didn't sound surprised about that.'

'Missing pets... Do you think they could have been stolen?'

I stopped walking too. Partly so I could turn to Jess in a dramatic way and partly because I was out of breath from walking up the hill. 'Stolen animals!'

'So maybe the van that hit the deer was full of stolen pets, as well as animals taken from sanctuaries and rescue centres.'

'And maybe the person driving it was The Rattler.'

'But if that's true, The Rattler and The Storm can't be working together. And where is he or she taking the animals?' Jess said.

'If we find that out,' I said, 'we might have the key to solving this whole mystery.'

We'd reached the street that ran alongside the park so I took my phone out of my pocket to text my mum. She was probably coordinating the health and safety situation on my road, but no doubt she'd be checking for my message every five seconds, too.

'@ park,' I texted, followed by a tree emoji, a thumbs up, the happy cat face and the bloody syringe for a joke.

'I flipping love my phone,' I said.

'Oh, really? I hadn't noticed.'

And, at that moment, something shot through the air towards me, thwacking into the side of my head really hard and knocking my hat off. I may or may not have let out a girly scream. I stumbled backwards and my phone smashed down on to the pavement.

'Oh my God,' Jess yelled. 'We're under attack!'

We moved closer together as the area around

us filled with squirrels. They clung to tree trunks, scurried across branches and stalked the ground at our feet. There must have been twenty of them, with a couple of really thuggish-looking ones standing between me and my phone.

'Are you alright?' Jess said. 'Your ear is bleeding.'

I put my hand up to my face and felt something wet and sticky. My fingers were red with blood. 'Oh no, not my farting ear! What if they've broken it?'

'We have bigger things to worry about, Alex.'

'OMG, you're right – my phone!'

'No, I meant the squirrels. I don't think they're done with us yet.'

'Try talking to them,' I said. 'It's our only hope.'

Jess began to twitch. 'Why are you doing this?' she shouted in between shudders. 'We aren't your enemy.'

'Can you ask them if I could just grab my phone back, please?'

The squirrels snarled at me.

'I'll take that as a no.'

Jess twitched to a stop, shook her head and put her hands up.

'Are we surrendering?' I said.

'Trust me, it's for the best.'

'But Jess,' I whispered. 'They're only squirrels – we can take them.'

The squirrels chattered – it was like they were laughing – and three of them scampered towards my phone.

'Ah, they're getting my phone back for me,' I said. 'You see that, Jess? I intimidated them with my courage and air of authority. They know who's in control of this situation.'

Jess said nothing, just raised an eyebrow.

'If you could just bring it here carefully, guys,' I said to the squirrels. 'I can see a small crack on the screen but that's no biggy – I'm sure it will still work fine.'

The squirrels looked up at me and then started pushing my phone in the opposite direction.

'Erm, that's the wrong way,' I said.

The squirrels ignored me and kept pushing. I started to move towards them so I could get my phone back, but another squirrel leapt from a nearby tree, just skimming past my face, followed by another and another. They landed right in front of me and gnashed their teeth.

'Do you think they bite?' I said.

'Probably,' Jess said.

'I'm not getting my phone back, am I?'

'Nope.'

The squirrels knocked my phone off the kerb into the road, their bushy tails bobbing around. And then they kicked it. Straight down the drain.

'Nooooooooooooo!' I cried, falling to my knees. It was kind of like Darth Vader in *Revenge of the Sith*, except my situation was far worse than his. He'd lost his wife and baby. I'd lost my brand new iPhone.

'Our photos!' Jess said. 'We've lost the only evidence we had.'

The squirrels laughed again and then, as quickly as they'd appeared, they were gone, leaving just a rustling in the trees.

'What the hell was that?' I said.

'That was a warning.' Jess bent down and picked up my hat for me. 'We're to stop interfering.'

'Or what? They've taken my phone. What else can they do?'

'Quite a lot, it seems. They have big plans. And if we try to stop them…' Jess looked dead serious, her blue eyes wide.

'What?'

'The Storm Is Coming,' she said. 'For us.'

# 10

## Falling Out With Jess

So let's just say that my mum went absolutely mental when I got home. The scraped arm, the cut ear and the missing phone equalled Mum overload. To the max. The only good thing was that she was so upset about my injuries and so busy talking to the local news people who came to ask her about the 'incident', that she forgot to be cross about the phone. She even talked about keeping me off school the next day. Normally I would have been all over that, but I was desperate to get back to the sanctuary to see if Mr Prickles was OK. No school would mean no animal sanctuary, so I told her I was fine to go in.

At lunchtime on Monday, me and Jess went to see The Professor.

'I must say that this is all astonishing,' Miss Fortress said. 'I've never heard of animals behaving that way before. I'm no expert but it doesn't seem natural.'

'We actually know an expert.' Jess looked down and scratched at the table. 'And he says the same – that the animal behaviour is abnormal, but nobody really knows why.'

I couldn't help it – I had to say something. 'I don't see why we should believe what he says though.'

'Shut up, Alex. You don't know what you're talking about.'

'Excuse me, but am I not a human lie detector?'

'Yes, but…'

'And did my right ear not fart when Taran was talking?'

'So you say.'

'Are you accusing me of lying?' I knew Jess didn't want to believe Taran had lied, but I couldn't believe that she would accuse me of making it up.

'I wouldn't know, would I?' Jess glared at me.

'What's this?' Miss Fortress looked between the two of us and stuffed some raspberry and white chocolate muffin into her mouth.

'Conflict of interests,' I said. 'Jess has got too close to a suspect and her obvious crush on Taran is compromising the mission.' I know it was harsh but I was so mad at her.

'How dare you?' Jess shrieked and launched herself at me.

I wouldn't usually have been scared in that situation, but because I was already suffering from extreme injuries that impaired my reflexes and fighting ability, I thought my best course of action was to run away. So I skidded across the room, putting a couple of tables and plenty of chairs between me and Jess.

'Jess! Alex!' Miss Fortress shouted. 'Stop this at once!' She didn't bother to get up, though – she really was the most inadequate teacher I'd ever come across.

'Can't you give Jess a bit of my power, Miss?' I said. 'Then she'd know I was telling the truth. And, come to think of it, I wouldn't mind having some of hers so she's not the only person who can talk to animals. I'm sick of her thinking she's better than me.'

'You're just jealous because I can understand Mr Prickles and you can't.'

'Mr Prickles and me have an understanding that transcends words!' I yelled. 'And you wouldn't know anything about it because you hate everybody and everything.'

'Now there's a thought,' Miss Fortress said, leaning forward on the table, her chin in her hand. She had a smear of muffin on her cheek but I didn't like to say anything.

'What thought?' Jess and me said at the same time.

'I wonder if there's a way of connecting you both, so that you can receive each other's brain transmissions.'

'So we could get a bit of each other's power you mean?' Jess sniffed.

'Exactly.' Miss Fortress smiled. 'I do like a challenge.'

'Is it even possible?' I said.

'Yes – in theory. But we'll never know for sure unless we try.'

'So you want to experiment on us again,' said Jess.

'It'll be fun!' Miss Fortress jumped out of her chair and grabbed a pile of papers and books from a cupboard behind her desk. She was muttering to herself and seemed to have forgotten we were there.

'Should we go then?' I said.

She just waggled her hand.

Me and Jess didn't talk to each other for the rest of the day at school. We walked to the animal sanctuary separately, though I made sure I got there first because I am a winner and these things are important. I went straight to enclosure 17 and I was so relieved to see Mr Prickles waiting for me. I picked him up and gave him a hug and told him all about my argument with Jess. Mr Prickles is a very good listener, FYI.

'What's that, Mr Prickles?' I said, tickling his cute little paws with their soft leathery skin. 'You think I should prove to Jess that she's wrong by conducting my own rogue investigation?'

Mr Prickles wriggled in my hand.

'That is a brilliant idea. You're a genius.'

When I went back into the building, Jess was preparing the bowls of food. Her anger seemed to have spread to her hair because it was extra wild. She looked like a blonde Bellatrix.

'I'll do outside, you do inside?' I said.

'Why should you get to do outside?' she shouted, her face bright pink.

'Calm down, Jess. You'll disturb the nest of rabid birds that live in your hair. I'll do inside if you're going to make a thing of it.'

She grabbed some bowls and stomped off into the garden.

What she didn't know is that I'd wanted to do inside. I'd used my years of agent experience in trickery and deception and made her think that I'd wanted to do outside, knowing that then *she'd* want to do outside. She'd played right into my hands.

I should probably flashback to thirty minutes earlier, when I ran as fast I could to get to the sanctuary before her. I'm pretty sure Rex and his mum weren't expecting me, because when I got there I walked in on something I'd really rather forget. Rex was sitting on a chair and his mum was standing behind him. She was wearing this weird glove that was covered in metal bristles, and – I can hardly bear to say it – she was *grooming* him. She was brushing his hair, like he was a dog. It was the worst thing I'd ever seen in my life, except for the time my mum drank too much wine at our Christmas party and fell over and all our neighbours saw her pants. Anyway, before they noticed me standing there, I overheard a bit of their conversation.

Rex's mum said, 'The animal behaviourist is arriving at 4pm.'

'I'll see him, Mum. You must be tired.'

'Can I rely on you to make the necessary arrangements? You've been a disappointment of late.'

'I won't let you down, Mum.'

'Good boy, Rex.'

Then they saw me, and it's probably better if I never relive that moment. Let's just say it was awkward.

Fast forward to 3:55 and I was desperate to get away from Jess and do some investigating at the front of the sanctuary where I knew Taran would be.

I slunk through the building like a slinky thing, slipped behind the storeroom door and waited.

From my hiding place I could hear everything that went on in the reception area. Soon afterwards, the door buzzer rang and I heard Rex walk down the corridor to the front door.

'Taran,' he said. From anyone else, I'd think that was quite a rude greeting, but Rex wasn't known for being Mister Friendly-Pants.

'Hey there, Rex.' I could hear the smile in Taran's voice. I imagined his cool hair and conker-brown eyes and it made me mad that he was so nice-slash-handsome.

'We'll talk in the infirmary,' said Rex.

Fudge it, I was hoping I'd be able to listen to their conversation and pick out some lies, but the infirmary was the little room where they kept all the animal medicines and stuff. It had glass windows all the way around so you could see in and out. I'd never be able to sneak up on them in there.

They walked down the corridor and turned left towards the infirmary. I could only hear Rex and Taran. I listened for the click of Meena's claws on the tiles but she definitely wasn't there.

I was about to say a lot of swears under my breath and go back to do the actual jobs that I was there to do when I had a thought. The animal-abducting van! I could sneak outside and see if Taran had a van parked in the lane.

I let myself out of the front door as quietly as possible and made my way down the path to the gate. I was a bit worried about people on the street seeing me in my overalls, especially as there was a news crew down the road, taking photos of another sinkhole. But the mission came first.

After I'd closed the gate behind me, I glanced up and down the road, looking for a van. There were a lot of parked cars, but no van. I was really disappointed, but I decided to take a reccy anyway. I turned right first, in the opposite direction to the school, looking into every car I passed. I tried to do it kind of casually because I didn't want people to think I was a car thief or something. I was about four cars down when I saw a familiar face. It was Meena.

'Hey, Meena,' I said, tapping on the window. I'm a bit scared of dogs sometimes, but Meena always acted like she wouldn't hurt anybody. She jumped up on the seat and wagged her tail. The car she was in wasn't a van. It was a brand new bright blue Mini Countryman. The licence plate said T8R8N 1.

So much for Taran being The Rattler. I'd been so sure he wasn't what he seemed. But as I peeped in through the window, I noticed something that was going to prove to Jess what a big fat liar he was.

Meena started whining at me, like she was trying to say something.

'I'm sorry, Meena, I can't understand you like Jess can,' I said. 'I've got to go now, but I'll see you soon.' I gave her a wave and then raced back to the sanctuary.

'Jess!' I said, trying to catch my breath. 'He's been lying to you.'

'Who has?' She gave me a filthy look.

'Taran. I have something to tell you about him.'

'What is it, Alex?' For a moment her face looked less ferocious than it had all day. She was going to be so grateful when I told her, and apologise to me a gazillion times.

'Brace yourself, Jess. Taran isn't a vegan. His car is full of McDonalds wrappers.'

'You what?' Jess said.

'He lied to you. He's not a vegan. He eats chicken nuggets.'

I smiled, waiting for Jess to thank me and

maybe even hug me, which is something that she never does.

Instead she turned and walked off.

'What's wrong?' I ran after her. 'I knew he was lying and I just risked my life to find out the truth for you.'

'You didn't find out the truth for me,' she shouted. 'You spied on him to prove a stupid point and to make him look bad. Sometimes you're such a jerk.' She stormed across the garden, spilling food out of the bowls she was carrying, her too-big overalls making her look like a nursery kid throwing a tantrum.

I didn't bother following her.

# 11

## Things Get Super-Creepy

Jess got her mum to pick her up at the end of her shift, so I went home and sat in my kitchen alone. Well, not alone, exactly, I had Bob and Elle to keep me company. It felt strange not having Jess there, eating her nasty-looking soy-based snacks and complaining about my freestyle rapping. More importantly, we couldn't talk through our mission status together. I was so mad with her, but the more I thought about it, the more I realised something: I missed her

After dinner I sat with my back to the kitchen window, going through a decorating magazine with Belle, (Belle was Bob and Elle's ship name, though Bob didn't like it because it wasn't symmetrical). It was even more boring than usual because I didn't have anyone to chat to while I was turning the pages. Also, it was really hard to know when Belle wanted me to go to the next page, or if they were just excited about a potted fern.

I'd been slowly dying of boredom for about thirty minutes when I saw something reflected on the countertop. My heart stopped. It was that in-between time of day, when you need the lights on to look at stuff properly, but it's not quite dark outside so the blinds on the windows aren't closed yet. There was a dim light shining through the kitchen window behind me, making the window's outline reflect on the shiny counter surface. I stared at that rectangle of light until I was sure. It was shadowy and I couldn't make out the detail, but I was certain. There was a face at the window, watching me.

I wished even harder that Jess was there – she always made me feel much braver. I held my breath and slowly turned on my stool, just in time to catch a movement at the window. The face was gone. The kitchen light flickered and went off, making everything seem creepily dark.

I heard Lauren call Mum from somewhere in the house.

'Don't worry, sweetheart, it's just another power cut!' Mum shouted back. 'Alex, are you OK?'

'Yeah, Mum!' I said, even though my heart was racing.

'Stay put for a sec. I'll sort Lauren out and then bring you some candles.'

So I sat on my stool, telling Belle everything was going to be fine while I stared at the window and the world grew blacker around me. By the time Mum came down, it was properly dark.

She lit a few candles and made sure I was OK, then she went in the living room to phone the electric company.

I knew what I had to do.

I picked up my Kylo Ren lightsaber and let myself out of the front door as quietly as I could. I looked both ways and strained my ears, listening to the shadows around me. I couldn't see or hear anything. I turned on my lightsaber, partly to scare off any murderers hiding in the bushes, and partly for the light. Also, it makes a really cool noise. I squeezed past the hedge and felt my way across the front of the house to the kitchen window. Using the light from my weapon, I scanned the ground beneath me. I couldn't see any footprints or anything that the window-watcher might have dropped. It was annoying, because bad guys always drop gum or something on TV, which you can get DNA from to uncover their identity. I was about to give up when the red light from my saber flashed over the wall under the window.

I jumped back, my stomach flipping up into my ribcage.

Scratched into the brickwork was some writing. And you might think you can guess what it said, but you'd be wrong. It didn't say 'The Storm Is Coming', it said something much more frightening. It said 'The Storm Is Here'.

I got to school early on Tuesday so I could wait for Jess. I really needed to see her. But when I turned on to Cherry Tree Lane, I could see her already standing outside the school gate. I was a bit worried it was so she could kick me in the boy bits, but as

I got closer, her face didn't look angry. I walked towards her and stopped about a metre away.

'You want to walk in together?' she said.

'Sure.'

We walked in silence for a minute. I'd planned what I wanted to say to Jess when I saw her, but now it felt weird.

'I'm sorry, Alex,' she said, without looking over at me. 'You were right – I should have paid attention when Taran lied, and I know you would never say he had if he hadn't. I was being an idiot.'

I nearly fainted. 'Are you messing with me?'

'No, I mean it.'

'Yeah, well, I shouldn't have gone behind your back and I definitely shouldn't have said those horrible things to you. I'm sorry too. Friends again?'

Jess smiled. 'Definitely.'

'Good, because not being friends with you sucked.'

'Same,' she said.

We were the first people in the school playground so we had it all to ourselves.

'Let's dibs the climbing frame,' I said and we ran over to it, chucking our school bags at the bottom and climbing up the ramp to the bridge in the middle. We sat down on it and dangled our legs over the side, watching our breath come out in cold white puffs.

'Mission update?' Jess said.

'Defos. You go first.'

'Yesterday after our argument, I caught Rex coming out of the office. When he saw me, he quickly put something in his pocket. I asked him about it and he said he was fetching something for his mum. But because you weren't there, I couldn't tell if he was lying or not.'

'Interesting,' I said. 'So annoying that I wasn't there to help you. And I could have done with your help when I went out to look for Taran's car. I'm sure Meena was trying to talk to me.'

'Two missed opportunities.'

'Wait till you hear what happened last night,' I said, and I filled Jess in on my sinister stalker and the message he left on the wall.

'Are you OK? That sounds pretty scary.'

'You know me, Jessticles. I have nerves of steel.' I nudged her with my elbow. 'But it would have been better if you were there.'

'We work best as a team,' said Jess.

'So we stick together from now on.'

'Always.' She held her little finger up to me.

'I thought we were friends now, Jess – why are you giving me some kind of weird finger swear?'

'Double-O-Divvy,' she said, nudging me back.

'I think you mean Double-O-Delightful.'

We sat on the climbing frame, chatting and laughing. It felt great after all the stressing at each other – I guess we'd both been struggling with our own worries.

The view from the top of the climbing frame was pretty that freezing November morning. Everything was covered in frost that sparkled in the sunlight. I turned my head and looked across the field to the vegetable garden.

'Jess, look,' I said. 'Can you see that?'

She turned and looked. 'Is that what I think it is?'

We both stood up to get a better view. At the far end of the school field there was a group of animals – dogs, cats, a rabbit and what looked like a bunch of rats. Not fighting or chasing each other; sitting in a circle like they were best mates.

'Are they having a meeting?' I said.

'Normally I'd say that wasn't possible,' said Jess. 'But that's really what it looks like.'

'How much chance do you reckon we have of getting over there without them running away?'

'About zero. They'll hear us, see us and smell us before we get a quarter of the way across the field.'

'Remember I'm super-stealthy, Jess.'

'Remember you also stink.'

'But nobody's lied!'

'I know, but animals have much more sensitive noses than we do and, honestly, your stink kind of lingers.'

I tugged my hat down a bit lower. 'We should at least try though, right?'

'Yeah, I guess so.'

We ran down the ramp and moved quietly through the playground to the edge of the field.

'YOLO,' I said and started sprinting as fast as I could towards the animal meeting. The cold air seared through my chest, and the icy grass crunched underneath my feet. One section of the field dips down and then slopes upwards, and trying to run up it made my legs burn. We lost sight of the animals for a few seconds, as we descended into the dip, and when the garden came into view again, the animals were gone.

'I think I'm going to die.' I bent over, gasping for air.

'They've not even left any clues. There's nothing here. Nothing!' Jess sat on the wall of the vegetable patch.

'I didn't see any people, though, did you? Nobody who could be The Storm or The Rattler.'

'No. Definitely just animals.'

'Oh, look,' I said, noticing the fence behind the vegetable patch for the first time. 'The school field joins up to the animal sanctuary. We could climb over the fence instead of walking all the way there. Like a short-cut.'

'It's like five minutes away, Alex – you're so lazy sometimes. And isn't it weird that the animal meeting was so close to the animal sanctuary? If only we'd managed to speak to the animals! They were right there! I feel like everything we need is close by but we're not quite able to reach it.'

'It felt like that with the PALS case, though, remember?' I sat down next to her.

'It did. And we cracked it.'

'We didn't just crack it, Jess. We smashed it.'

'I suppose we have learnt a lot since the last time we were at the vegetable patch,' Jess smiled.

'That's it!' I jumped up again. 'The last time we were at the vegetable patch it was because Boris and Noodle were here. A coincidence, Jessticles? I think not!'

# 12

## You Can't Keep a Secret From a Goldfish

At breaktime, we filled in Darth Daver on what we'd seen. He agreed that we needed to speak to Boris and Noodle. Unfortunately, Boris and Noodle lived in the nursery classroom and that was kept locked at all times. And not just a normal lock: one of those high-tech keypads that you need to know a number code for.

We'd hoped Miss Fortress would be able to help us with the code, but she'd been really distracted for the past week. In class it was like she couldn't be bothered to teach us anything, she just gave us tests. She was never around for me and Jess to speak to at lunch, unless it was 'a life or death emergency situation that only she could assist with and that wouldn't result in her compromising her secret identity'. Also, she 'didn't know the code for the nursery door and wasn't about to go poking around in other teachers' business in order to find out'.

'I don't know what her problem is,' Jess said. We were sitting on the Reflections Bench, trying not to freeze our butts off. 'If she thought all this was something to do with Montgomery McMonaghan and SPARC, I'm sure she'd be more helpful.'

In case you've forgotten, SPARC Industries is the company run by Montgomery McMonaghan, Miss Fortress's old lab partner turned super-villain. We were certain that he was behind all the PALS brainwashing at our school last half term, but we didn't have enough evidence to convince the authorities. Miss Smilie had taken the fall, and Montgomery McMonaghan had lived to fight another day.

'To be fair, if I had a nemesis with an evil

corporation like Montgomery McMonaghan, I'd probably get a bit obsessed with it too. Even though the PALS stuff is over, it doesn't mean he's not planning something else. Anyway, I think she's working on something sciencey. She's always scrabbling around in a pile of papers and fiddling with wires. And all the journalists loitering around because of the weird animal incidents are making her nervous in case her cover is blown. She looks even tireder and more mad than usual.'

'So how are we going to get the code for the nursery? I thought maybe we could ask Bob, but the only place to put him would be on the windowsill next to the door, and everyone would see him there.' She shoved her hands, which were turning a freaky shade of blue, under her jumper.

'You know what?' Dave said, taking off his gloves and giving them to Jess. 'Instead of hiding him, you could camouflage him. He could be right in front of people's eyes without them paying him any attention.'

'I'm listening, Gentle Genius,' I said. 'What did you have in mind?'

When we finished work at the sanctuary that night, Jess came over to my house so we could work on Bob together.

'All you need to do is peep at the keypad when someone's going in and remember the number,' Jess said, leaning over the breakfast bar.

'It's an easy task,' I said. 'It's so basic it's on page one of the AAAA handbook.'

Jess twitched for a bit. 'He wants to know why you don't do it yourself if it's so easy.'

'I totes would, but I'm like a celebrity since I saved the school from certain doom. My profile is so high that I would definitely be noticed.'

Bob, Elle and Jess looked at me like I was a maggot in their dinner.

'I thought you liked being an agent,' I said. 'You've not been out of your tank since you took on Miss Smilie. Don't you want a mission?'

Jess gave me a look. 'Take some time to think it over, Bob.'

I was very confused. Why would Bob need time to think it over? I grabbed Jess's phone, typed out a message and slid it back to Jess. It said, '*confused face emoji* ? *fish emoji* nd to *thought bubble emoji* ?'

Jess frowned and wrote a message back. 'Bob *scream face emoji* ? Not left *house emoji* since *smiley emoji* *T-shirt emoji* *splashes emoji*'

I nodded and typed another message. '*monkey covering eyes emoji* nrly *skull emoji* *skull and crossbones emoji* *coffin emoji*'

Jess started to twitch.

'What is it?'

'He said he knows we're talking about his death through cartoon picture code.'

You can't get anything past that fish. I turned to him. 'Before you make your decision, Bob, I should just tell you that there aren't any evil psychopath teachers at our school anymore. I suspected Miss Hussein for a while, but she's annoyingly nice.'

'It's relatively risk free,' Jess said, followed by some twitching. 'No, I can't promise you that you won't get a headache.' She twitched again. 'A couple of hours, tops.'

She side-eyed me. 'But we don't want to put pressure on you. We can find another way.' Jess picked up the fish-tank catalogue we'd got for Belle and let it fall open on a page full of luxury fish habitats. 'This one's nice, don't you think?'

Was Jess being manipulative? I was shocked!

Bob looked from Jess, to the page of tanks, to me, then to Elle.

Jess twitched. 'That's great, thanks Bob.' She gave me a thumbs-up.

We planted a cunningly disguised Bob on the windowsill the next morning. He was in his usual jar (after he watched us wash it out about a hundred times to make sure there was no trace of energy drink), but we'd wrapped the jar in a cardboard cylinder that we made ourselves, leaving a small hole for Bob to peep through. Dave printed us out a label that said 'Cherry Tree Lane Science Experiment – PLEASE DO NOT TOUCH'. He put the school badge on it so it looked like one of the teachers had printed it. We put the jar on the windowsill with a mirror behind it so if anyone gave it a second glance, they'd think we were studying the effect of sunlight on water or something like that. So he was where everyone could see him, but we were confident that nobody would move him.

'Good luck, Agent Bob,' I whispered as we quietly left the corridor. 'We'll be back at lunch.'

The nursery is closed at lunchtime after the morning kids have gone home and before the afternoon kids arrive, so we had a small window to get Bob, get the code, talk to the guinea pigs and get out. It was a lot to fit in and it meant sacrificing some of our eating time, so it wasn't the best.

After checking that the coast was clear, we snuck down the corridor towards the nursery entrance and I was relieved to see that Bob's jar was where we left it.

'Did you get the code, Bob?' I said.

Jess gave me one of her fiercest looks. 'Firstly, Bob, are you OK in there?'

She started to shake around, particularly on the left side of her body, which looked very funny. 'Oh God, sorry Bob,' she said, grabbing the mirror and turning it to face the other way.

'What's wrong?' I said.

'Um, the mirror's been reflecting the sunlight on to his jar this whole time. He's a bit hot and a lot grumpy.'

I bit my lip so I wouldn't laugh. 'Just think of it as a nice warm bath,' I said. 'Mum always says they can make anything feel better.'

'He said if it was summer he would have been cooked,' Jess said. 'And he has a headache.'

'Sorry, Bob. We'll get you back home as soon as we can. Please give us the code and then we can get out of here.'

Jess twitched again. 'Thank you, Bob. We won't be long.'

'Ooh, can I press the buttons?' I said.

'What's that all over your hands?'

I was glad she asked. 'It's a special sealant that I painted over my fingertips so that I won't leave fingerprints on the entry pad. I got the formula from the Agent Academy handbook.'

'It's dried glue, isn't it?'

'Of course not,' I said, and my ear puffed.

'Go ahead,' Jess stood aside, 'if it means that much to you. The code is 1925.'

'That must be the year that Mrs Kimmeny was born,' I said. Mrs Kimmeny was the nursery teacher and she was the oldest person I'd ever seen outside of my mum's Zumba class, which was full of grannies who were too old to have jobs but not too old to jiggle about in inappropriate sportswear.

'Just put the code in,' Jess sighed.

'You're supposed to say, "punch it, Agent Alex."'

'Not saying it.'

'Then we'll be here all lunch until we get caught.'

Jess put her hands on her hips.

I tapped my gluey fingers on the wall.

'Fine! Punch it, Agent Alex. Also, I hate you.'

'Affirmative! Prepare to enter hyperspace.' I entered the code, leaving bits of glue crust on the keypad. The code pad was disappointingly silent, so I added some beeping noises as I pressed the buttons. I pulled the handle and the door opened.

'Are you doing sound effects now?'

'Just trying to add a bit of excitement, Jessticles.'

'You're going to get us caught.'

'Hey, I have the perfect sound effect for you – it goes like this...' I made the loudest, wettest fart noise possible.

Jess muttered something about me being immature but I couldn't really hear because I was moving at warp speed into the nursery (with sound effects).

Boris and Noodle's hutch was in the corner of the room next to the back door that led to the nursery playground.

'Boris! Noodle! Come out please,' Jess said. 'We need to talk to you.'

Noodle's curly-haired face appeared at the doorway, and Jess started to twitch.

'I don't care if Boris's appointments are closed for the day, I need a word.'

'How does a guinea pig have appointments?' I said. 'Is there a sign-up sheet?' I put my face close to the hutch. 'Do you have a secretary we can phone, Boris?'

'He's just trying to avoid talking to us,' Jess frowned. 'Come out, Boris or I'll come in.'

I assessed the hutch and, to be fair, Jess probably could fit in it. But there was a rustle inside and Boris emerged, with a face on him like he couldn't imagine what we wanted to talk to him about.

'The Storm,' Jess said. She was in proper no-nonsense mode. 'What do you know?'

She juddered about for a couple of minutes, occasionally asking questions, like 'Have you met him yourself?' and 'How do I know you're telling the truth?'

I found those minutes so painful. Can you imagine what it's like to have to stand around not knowing what's going on while your sidekick finds out all the juicy secrets? It totally sucks.

Finally Jess went back to normal and Boris disappeared into the depths of his hutch.

'So?' I said.

'Let's get out of here first, and then I'll tell you.'

'What are you two doing in here?' a voice said from behind us. For a moment I had a flashback of Miss Smilie with her sharky face, but when I turned round I saw Miss Hussein.

I had to think fast.

'Hello, Miss Hussein,' I said. 'Me and Jess came in here for a good reason, actually. We heard one of the nursery kids saying the guinea pigs were poorly, and you know me and Jess volunteer at the animal sanctuary? We work there nearly every day for free, because we care about the animals so much. And so we thought we could help the guinea pigs. We didn't want them to suffer, you see.'

My ear was dropping fart bombs like crazy.

'So we came in here and saw that they *are* ill with some kind of stomach bug. Honestly, there is so much poo. And not the good solid kind. So we were helping them because, you know, we care and we're nice people.'

Miss Hussein gave me one of her twinkliest smiles. 'That's so lovely of you,' she said. 'You two are always doing good deeds – helping other children, looking after the guinea pigs – you're assets to the school.'

Jess just stood there, looking shifty, so I grabbed her arm and started pulling her towards the door. 'I'm sorry we came in here without permission, Miss. We just thought it was an emergency and we couldn't find a teacher.'

'Oh goodness, someone must have left the door open.' Miss Hussein turned to fiddle with the lock.

'Would you like us to get Mr Crumpet to have a look at it?' I said.

'No, thank you. Let's not bother him on his lunch break. I'll see if I can sort it out. You two had better go and enjoy the rest of your playtime.'

'Thanks, Miss Hussein,' I said, pushing Jess out of the door in front of me. She picked up Bob's jar and we walked away.

'Still think she's evil?' I couldn't see Jess's face but I could tell it was smug.

The only thing I could do was change the subject. 'What did you find out from Boris?'

'Not as much as I wanted, and I'm not even sure

if he was telling the truth or not. The thing with Boris is that he takes care of himself before anyone else. He likes to be on the winning team and has zero loyalty, so he can't be trusted.'

'So you didn't learn anything useful?'

'I wouldn't say that, but I wouldn't be surprised if news of our chat gets back to The Storm.'

'So he's a double-agent?' I said.

'No, he's just a jerk.'

'Does he know The Storm?'

'He's never met him. The last time he and Noodle escaped, they were going to meet The Storm but then it started raining. Boris doesn't like the rain, so when we came along, he decided his best option was to go back to the hutch.'

'Then he must know about him at least?'

'He does, but he wouldn't say much. I think he's scared of him. He said everybody's scared of him. I did find out one useful thing, though.'

'You know, you're really dragging this out. Tell me!'

'The Storm isn't a human. He's an animal.'

'*What*?' I wasn't expecting that. 'Then why is everyone so afraid? And how has he got so many different animals working together?'

'All Boris would say is that something happened to him in his past – something that made him different. He was treated badly by humans, and now he has only one purpose in life.'

'He has a backstory? I love a tragic backstory. He sounds like a proper G. What is his purpose in life?'

We'd reached my classroom, where we were going to stash Bob for the rest of the day. Jess stopped and looked at me.

'Revenge.'

# 13

## Chasing the Storm

We had to get Bob straight home after school, so we told Rex we were feeling unwell and couldn't work at the sanctuary. I was disappointed because seeing Mr Prickles was my favourite part of the day but I totally got that Bob wanted to get back to his nice cool tank. Meanwhile, me and Jess tried to come up with ideas about how to find The Storm. Now that we knew he was an angry animal, we figured the best thing we could do would be to speak to him and try to find out why he had such a crazy thirst for vengeance.

'We could ask Jason's dog?' I said.

Jess turned a page of the magazine in front of Bob's tank and shook her head. 'Look, Bob – here's that page on feature walls.' Then she turned back to me. 'She was the rudest, most vicious dog I've ever met – there's no way she'd tell us anything. And anyway, I overheard Jason saying she's run away.'

'Another lost pet,' I said. 'Interesting. Oh, Bob – I found the article on north-facing gardens you were looking for.'

'The squirrels won't tell us anything either,' Jess said.

'And we don't even know what he looks like. He could be standing right in front of us and we'd have no clue.'

'Yes, Elle, it says that stone pillar comes in a vintage marble finish,' said Jess. 'I wonder what kind of animal he is.'

'He's probably something bad-A, like a sabre-tooth tiger. And this is the pump that boosts the oxygen level in the water by 3.8 percent.'

'Do you not think people might have noticed him if he was a sabre-tooth tiger? Besides, I'm pretty sure they're extinct.'

'An elephant then,' I said.

'That's £399.99, Bob. Even with a junior discount, I don't think we can stretch to that. Don't be ridiculous, Alex.'

'Maybe a wolf? That would be so cool.'

'We'll never know if we can't work out how to find him,' said Jess. 'Hold up, Bob's saying something.' She went into full twitch mode.

'Was he asking about that imported Japanese tank grass again?' I said.

'No, he actually had an idea. He said that seeing as The Storm has already taken an interest in us, watching through the window and sending us warnings, we don't need to look for him.'

'We don't?'

'Bob says that if we ruffle enough feathers, The Storm will come to us.'

From then on, we took every opportunity to poke our noses into The Storm's business. Luckily, or unluckily, depending which way you looked at it, there were more and more strange incidents occurring around town. We had power cuts twice a day; there were loads of car accidents due to roads collapsing; there were squirrel muggings and dogs vandalising property. It was getting out of control. And whenever me and Jess came across another animal anomaly, or as I liked to call them, animalomaly, we interfered. We interviewed every animal we could find, we measured holes, we climbed trees and we photographed everything (on Jess's phone, not mine obvs because that was floating down a drain tunnel somewhere). We even printed a map of the area and put stickers on all the places that the animalomalies occurred.

And every day we went to the animal sanctuary to spy on Rex and keep watch over the animals.

It was a Monday, and we'd been working at the sanctuary for about three weeks. During that time, only Sir Blimmo had been taken, so the atmosphere there was pretty tense. It seemed only a matter of time until The Rattler claimed his next victim.

I would never admit it to Jess, but I was loving my time there. As often as I could, I left Jess to do the dirty work and I went to hang out with Mr Prickles. I was hoping that, once the case was over, we'd be able to find a way to be together. I'd started putting the groundwork in with my mum about maybe getting a new pet and I was actually making good progress. I thought about it as me and Jess walked to the sanctuary after school.

'Are you humming?' Jess said.

'No. Maybe.'

'I heard you humming that at the sanctuary the other day, too. What is it?'

'Just a song.' I tried to make my face look innocent.

'Oh my God,' Jess stopped in the middle of the street and grabbed my arm. 'You have a song for Mr Prickles, don't you?'

'Of course not,' I said. My ear farted and Jess wrinkled her nose. 'But if I did, I don't see why that would be such a bad thing.'

'This is brilliant.' She was jiggling up and down on the spot like she needed a wee. 'What song is it?'

'I don't want to say.'

'Please tell me — I'll never ask anything of you again if you tell me.'

'It's the one from *Tangled* where they're sitting in the boat and all the lanterns are lighting up the sky.'

Jess looked at me and made a weird face where she was kind of sucking her cheeks in and biting her lip at the same time. It looked like she was in pain.

'Are you OK?' I said.

She nodded and kept making the face.

'Are you trying not to laugh?'

She swallowed, took a deep breath and said, 'Alex Sparrow. This is the best. Thing. Ever.' And then she laughed, harder than I've ever seen her laugh before.

When we got to the sanctuary, the first thing I noticed was the most awful stink, and for once it wasn't coming from me.

'Oh God,' said Jess, looking at me.

'It wasn't me!' I said. 'It's coming from inside.'

We opened the front door and the evil smell poured through, filling our noses like we were drowning in stink. Rex was standing at the toilet door with a mop and bucket.

'What's going on?' Jess said.

'Drains are blocked. Toilet's flooded. Keep mopping while I change my shoes.'

I looked down at Rex's feet to see he was wearing fancy new trainers. They were shiny white and he was being very careful to keep them away from the puddle that was oozing out of the bathroom.

Jess took the mop. 'I wonder how this happened? Get the door for me, will you?'

I pushed the door and it swung open to reveal a room full of wee, poo, and…

'Frogs!' I said. 'What?' They were sitting on the toilet seat, splashing about in the puddle and hopping on the windowsill. There was even one wrapping himself in toilet paper.

'They must be working for The Storm,' Jess said. 'They've blocked the drains and clogged the toilet.'

'Gross,' I said. 'If I ever get a job with The Storm, I'm going to ask to be a ninja squirrel. There's no way he'd get me to go crawling around the sewers.'

But Jess wasn't listening, she was twitching and the frogs were ribbitting.

I heard a noise behind us. 'Rex is coming,' I said.

'You can do your usual jobs,' Rex said, taking the mop from Jess as if a room full of frogs was a totally normal thing.

'Has this happened before?' I asked.

'Couple of times.'

'Don't you think it's a bit weird?'

Rex just shrugged. He was so hard to get information from. I tried a new direction.

'Nice trainers. They look the same as Jason's. Did you manage to keep them clean?'

'Mostly.'

'Are they new?'

'Not really.' *Lie.*

'Bet they cost a lot of money.'

'Got them on sale.' *Lie.*

'They must have been expensive, still. Jason was bragging that his were a hundred quid. Does your mum pay you for working here?'

Rex dipped the mop in the bucket and squeezed the water out. 'Yeah.' *Lie.*

'Are you alright, Rex? You look a bit uncomfortable.'

'I'm fine.' *Lie.*

'So do you mind if we ask your mum if she'll pay us, too? I'll say that as she pays you it seems only fair.'

'Don't ask her,' Rex looked up.

'Why not?' I said. 'We've got nothing to lose by asking, and I'd really like a pair of those trainers myself. I expect when I tell her how much they are, she'll be happy to pay me.'

Rex looked totally freaked. 'Don't talk to her about my trainers. She won't understand. She doesn't think we should spend lots of money on clothes and stuff. She doesn't know what it's like at school being the outcast.'

He wasn't lying.

Rex was a suspect, and I was finally getting somewhere with him, but now I felt sorry for the guy. I wanted to carry on questioning him, but it seemed harsh to keep going when he was so obviously upset. I glanced at Jess and saw her shake her head, just a tiny bit.

'I guess we should feed the animals, then,' I said. 'They must be hungry.'

Rex just nodded and went back to mopping but I saw the look of relief flash across his face.

Maybe he was a bad guy who was drawn to the light side, like Kylo Ren. Or maybe he was a hero who looked like a beast and was shunned by society, like Nightcrawler. Or maybe he flipped between doing good deeds and naughty stuff, like Deadpool. There were so many possibilities. It was very confusing.

'Was Rex lying just now?' Jess said, when we got to the kitchen. 'I couldn't tell because, for the first time ever, I couldn't smell your ear farts.'

'Yeah, he was lying about everything except the last part. You know, the stuff about being an outcast.'

'That was sad. I think we should make more of an effort with him at school – he's always getting picked on.'

'We're so busy, though, Jess. We have the mission and, erm, stuff. And if we hang out with Rex, people might think we're the same as him.'

'For God's sake, Alex – have you learnt nothing from the past few months? It wasn't long ago that you were getting picked on. He needs a friend.'

'And are you forgetting that the reason we're questioning him is because he might already have a friend? A friend called … dramatic pause … The Rattler. He knows something, Jess.'

'Ugh, I don't remember our last mission being this confusing.' Jess slopped food into a bowl.

'You called it a mission!' I said. 'You're finally embracing the agent lifestyle.'

'Let's just get our jobs done.'

'Give me Mr Prickles's meaty chunks. Give 'em, give 'em, give 'em.'

'Take them,' she sighed, pushing the bowl towards me

I started walking to enclosure 17 – a.k.a. the

field of dreams – when the most flipping awful noise blared out across the garden. I was torn between going to investigate and taking Mr Prickles his food, but of course Mr Prickles won out. I ignored the noise and kept walking.

'We have to evacuate immediately,' Rex's voice yelled at me from somewhere back near the house. I kept walking.

'Alex! Stop!' he shouted again, and this time he came running up and grabbed me. 'Can't you hear that?'

'Hear what?' I said.

'Fire alarm.'

'Are you sure? I think it's just foxes. I've heard they make a sound very similar to a fire alarm.'

He looked at me like I was the biggest idiot on the planet. 'It's not foxes. It's the fire alarm. It's not a drill. We have to leave.'

'K, K,' I said. 'I'll just drop off this food…'

'That's against regulations,' Rex said. 'Put the bowl down and leave.'

Suddenly, I stopped feeling sorry for Rex. 'Make me.'

'Put the bowl down and get out or I'll have you and Jess fired.'

I thought for a moment. If Jess got fired, she'd never forgive me. If I got fired, I wouldn't see Mr Prickles again. And we'd never stop The Rattler. I had no choice. I put the bowl on the floor and walked off.

Mrs Fernandes gave me and Jess our bags, then pushed us towards the front door. 'I need to carry out a thorough inspection and ensure the safety of the animals,' she said. 'So you might as well go home.'

'Couldn't we help?' Jess asked.

'It's odd,' said Mrs Fernandes, 'that since you two started working here, problems have been continually cropping up.'

'You don't think we set off the alarm?' Jess said, looking at me as she said it, like she was wondering if it might have actually been me. I made a face at her.

'All I know is that people can't be trusted.'

'Hey – we've worked super hard here, and I can one hundred per cent confirm that neither of us set off the fire alarm,' I said. 'There have been weird incidents all over town lately, not just at the sanctuary. It's all over the news! There's no way we could be responsible for all of them.'

Mrs Fernandes thought for a second. 'You have done a reasonable job. You may return tomorrow, but I'll be watching you very closely.'

Great.

Just before we turned to leave, I saw Rex watching from the far end of the corridor. The front door slammed shut behind us, the alarm still blaring.

# 14

## The Fox Hunt

We stood outside the sanctuary gate, still dressed in our overalls.

'My mum is at work,' Jess said, looking at her phone. 'Should we call yours to ask her to pick us up?'

'It's too early. She'll be at dance club with Lauren. She won't be able to get us until after five.'

'So I guess we walk, then?'

It was a strange time to be out on the streets. All the school traffic was gone and none of the work traffic had started, so the roads were quiet and mostly empty. It was freezing cold and starting to get dark. There was a creepy atmosphere but I figured at least hardly anyone would see me in my overalls.

'I guess so.'

We turned left onto Cherry Tree Lane and headed towards the school.

'Do you think Rex set off the fire alarm?' I said.

'You mean to get rid of us? It's possible, I suppose. But there were the frogs, too, so it could have been another animal incident.'

'Would you please refer to them by their proper scientific name, Jessticles?'

'They don't have a proper scientific name.'

'You only say that because you weren't the genius who came up with animalomoly.'

'And I'll have to live with that regret for the rest of my life.' Jess pulled her backpack strap further up her shoulder. Her bag was nearly as big as she was.

'I've been thinking,' I said.

'Uh-oh.'

'We need eyes at the animal sanctuary. When we're there we're watched almost constantly, and I can't think of any plan that would allow us to stay there overnight.'

'Ha! You just want to have a sleepover with Mr Prickles. You could braid each other's hair and have midnight snacks of slugs and dog food.'

'Leave the jokes to me, Jess, they don't suit you,' I said, while picturing myself snuggled up in a sleeping bag in enclosure 17, laughing at funny YouTube clips with Mr P.

'So you want to ask Bob?'

'I think we should, don't you?'

Jess sighed. 'Yes. His services are getting so expensive, though. I've hardly got any money left.'

'You could sell your hair on eBay? I'm sure someone will pay good money for some hamster bedding.'

'We could ask Dexter to watch the sanctuary from the outside. If The Rattler comes, maybe he could follow the van and find out where The Rattler is taking the animals.'

'That's actually a brilliant idea,' I said. 'And we won't have to pay him, we'll just get The Professor to ask him to do it. He'll never say no to her.'

'Then we'll work on Bob tonight and ask Miss Fortress about Dexter tomorrow.'

We turned off Cherry Tree Lane on to Oak Avenue. It was never busy on Oak, but the road had been barricaded off due to half of it having crumbled away. The badgers or moles or whoever was making the holes around town had been extra busy in the side streets close to Cherry Tree Lane. By the time we got halfway down, the only sound we could hear was a bird chirping in one of the trees that lined the street. The light was fading fast but the streetlamps hadn't come on. I'm not going to lie, it was kind of spooky.

'That's a plan, then,' I said to break the silence.

'Feels weird being out at this time on our own,' said Jess, putting her hands in her coat pockets. 'Like we're not supposed to be here.'

'Yeah. And it's funny how different it looks. I've walked down this road a million times but it's like I've never been here before.'

Jess shivered. 'Not far now.'

As you know, I am exceptionally brave, but I have to admit that there is one person who is even slightly braver than I am, and that's Jess. Don't tell her I said that. I was glad I was with her.

'Maybe we should sing,' I said.

'Why?'

'Because someone very wise once told me that the best way to spread anti-fear is by singing loud for all to hear.'

'Alex, it's spreading *Christmas cheer*, and the person who said that was Buddy the Elf.'

'Meh, same thing. Let's try it.'

'Shush a minute.' Jess slowed to a stop and narrowed her eyes.

'What is it? Did you accidentally step on an ant? I've told you before, it happens to everyone – you shouldn't be too hard on yourself.'

'Shut up! I'm trying to listen! Can't you hear that?'

'Hear what?' I said, looking over my shoulder at the empty street behind us. There were no cars, no people, no lights and even the bird had stopped tweeting.

'I'm not sure, exactly – there's a noise getting louder, like it's moving towards us.'

We stood in silence, straining our ears, the shadows around us growing blacker and blacker.

'I think it's stopped. Maybe I imagined it,' Jess said as the streetlights flicked on one by one.

'Let's just go.' I was feeling super freaked out, and the thought of being at home in my warm, safe house was making me want to cry. And then I heard it, too – a high-pitched shriek that was somewhere between a scream and a howl. It was so awful that I didn't even bother trying to think of a mash-up word for it.

'Foxes,' Jess said.

'But that's like the most terrible sound I've ever heard in my life!' I said. 'How could that come from a fox?'

'Do you not remember the conversation we had a couple of weeks ago?'

'Nope.'

'The one where I said it was the most awful sound ever and you said it couldn't be that bad?'

'Definitely not,' I said. She knew I was lying, obvs.

There were a few seconds of silence, and I let out a deep breath. 'They're gone.'

Then the streetlights cut out and we were plunged into darkness. You know how when your mum turns your bedroom light off at night, and for a second you're totally blind before you start seeing a few blurry shapes again? At first it was like that. I couldn't see anything at all and I felt a massive surge of panic. Then Jess grabbed my hand. She'll tell you I grabbed her hand, but I'm pretty sure it was the other way around. After a second, I realised I could still see. The moon was bright and it wasn't full night yet.

The howling started again, louder and nearer.

'OMG, I literally jumped out of my skin,' I said.

'You didn't literally jump out of your skin. If you literally jumped out of your skin, your skin would be in a pile on the floor and you'd just be a bloody skeleton.'

'I know you're frightened, but there's no need for the swears, Jessticles.'

The foxes screamed again. They were close.

'They're saying something, in between the howling,' Jess said.

'Don't tell me – something about The Storm seeking a violent revenge on the human race?'

'Pretty much,' Jess said. 'Maybe we should run the rest of the way.'

But before we could take another step, we heard a clatter of claws on the pavement behind us. We turned around – afraid to look but knowing we had to – to see a pack of foxes pelting up the road towards us.

'Er, what are you supposed to do when you're

being chased by a bunch of foxes?' I said, backing away up the road. 'Is it one of those things where you're supposed to be all alpha-male and head towards them, growling?'

'I think, in this case, not.' Jess backed with me.

'So we run?'

'We run.'

We turned towards home and legged it down the street as fast as we could. Under normal circumstances, I could obviously out-pace a fox, but we were carrying huge bags full of school books and uniforms. I could tell the foxes were gaining on us. I could hear their panting and the scrape of their claws on the concrete.

'Don't look back, Alex,' Jess gasped.

'But we're not going to make it!' My heart was thudding, my mouth was dry and, even though it was about zero degrees outside, I was sticky with sweat.

'We can – we're almost there.'

Ahead I could see the place where Oak Avenue joined the main road. There were lights and cars and people. Surely we would be safe if only we could get just a bit further. I focused on the lights and the hum of traffic and poured every bit of my energy into my legs, making them pump harder and harder. My chest was burning, my lungs sucking in the freezing air, my heart throbbing at a hundred miles an hour. For one short, beautiful moment, I thought we were going to make it.

And that's when another pack of foxes skidded out on to the path in front of us.

We stumbled to a stop, gasping for air, and turned one way and then the other. Behind us, about twelve foxes were closing in. In front of us another eight were bombing in at top speed.

'We're surrounded,' I said, pulling Jess closer to me in the hope that the two of us together might look like one mighty, fox-resistant giant. 'Should we climb a tree?'

'There's no time.'

'Shout for help?'

'By the time someone comes, it will be too late.'

'Then there's only one choice,' I said, standing tall and puffing my chest out. 'We have to fight.'

A fox launched itself at us, mouth wide and snarling, spit dripping from its teeth. I froze for half a second, fear surging through my body and gluing it to the spot. And then I moved. You know how in movies, when a main character is about to be shot, or in this case bitten, the hero dives bravely in front of them and takes the hit? Well, I'd love to say this situation went down like that, but it didn't. In that moment I was a slave to my instincts. And my instincts told me to duck, and roll myself into a little ball on the concrete. I wasn't a complete coward, though, I did pull Jess down with me. The fox flew over us and crashed to the ground.

I tried to think what to do next – curling up on the floor wasn't going to work a second time. But then Jess stood up.

'Stop!' she said. 'We have to talk.'

The foxes formed a circle around us, their eyes glinting in the moonlight and their tails flicking across the ground. Even in the dark I could see they were all different colours – shades of orange, black and grey. There were small ones, no bigger than cats, and others that were much larger. But nearly all of them were skinny – I could see their bones through their fur.

'They look hungry,' I said. 'Foxes are vegetarian, right?'

'Sure. In opposite world.' Jess took a step forward and looked around the circle. 'Please wait. We're not your enemies. We only want to talk.'

Two foxes moved toward us and Jess started to twitch.

One of the fox leaders was big and mostly grey. He looked less bony than the others and I could see his muscles bulging in his shoulders and thighs. But I was less worried about him than I was about the fox next to him. He was probably the smallest in the pack – he looked starved. And he kept giving me dirty looks.

'We aren't all the same. If you could just ask The Storm to meet with us. I'm sure we can help each other,' Jess said in between zombie jerks.

'Jess,' I whispered. 'What's going on?'

'Kind of busy right now, Alex.'

'Tell me, tell me, tell me.'

Jess huffed and said to the foxes, 'Please excuse me one moment while I explain to my friend. He can't understand you like I can.'

Big grey fox dipped his head slightly. Small aggressive fox growled.

'OK,' said Jess. 'The grey fox is the leader of the foxes…'

'Is his name Arnold Foxenegger?'

Jess rolled her eyes. 'His name is General Pow, actually.'

'Also a cool name,' I nodded. 'Respect.'

'He commands the foxes on behalf of The Storm. He's been sent to give us one final warning to stay out of The Storm's business, or...'

'What's the little one saying?' The smaller fox was doing this snarly thing where he showed all of his teeth.

'She's saying "Bite. Bite. Let me bite the humans. Bite them."'

'Oh, that's not good,' I said. 'What's her name? Wait, let me guess – it's probably something like Fuzzykins or Sweetyfluff. The vicious animals in stories are always called cute names because it's hilariously ironic.'

'Her name is Biter.'

I watched as a blob of dribble splashed from Biter's lips to the floor. 'That works too.'

'As I was saying,' Jess sighed. 'The Storm says that if we don't stop getting involved in his business, asking questions and trying to find out his plans, we will be swept into a hurricane of suffering.'

'They already took my phone, what could be worse than that?'

Biter gnashed her teeth at me.

'Jess,' I whispered. 'Are they going to eat us?'

'Well, Biter certainly wants to. Can you let me go back to the negotiations now?'

'Sure. Nobody I'd trust more to negotiate for me. Negotiate well, my friend.'

Jess turned back to General Pow and Biter. 'I'm sorry, shall we continue?'

'If I could just make one small point?' I said.

The foxes turned to look at me.

'I'll take that as a "yes".' I did a karate bow to General Pow and tried not to stare at Biter's teeth. 'Greetings, friends. We mean you no harm.'

'They're foxes, not aliens, Alex,' Jess glared at me.

'Look. I realise there is some serious beef going down right now, and I don't blame you for being peed off. However, don't you think you're over-reacting just a tiny bit? With the howling, and the muggings, and the holes and stuff. You're taking it out on people who haven't done anything wrong.'

'General Pow says that this is a war and every war has casualties,' said Jess. 'Biter says she wants to bite you.'

A good agent knows how to read a potentially fatal situation and decides when to take a risk.

'If The Storm wanted you to eat us, you'd be chewing on our bones right now,' I said.

'Gross.' Jess screwed up her nose.

'You're not here to finish us, so there must be a chance for us to work things out. There is a man taking animals against their will. We want to stop him and we have vital information that can bring him down. You need us. Go back to your leader and tell him to parley with us on neutral ground.'

'Alex,' Jess whispered. 'You don't even know what parley means.'

'Nobody knows what parley means, Jessticles. It really doesn't matter.'

Jess did a bit of twitching and I waited, trying to look totes confident, even though I wasn't entirely feeling it.

Jess rolled her eyes. 'General Pow resents your rudeness but said he will relay our message.'

'*Yessssss!*' I said. 'And what about Biter? Did I win her over too? No one can resist the Alex Sparrow charm.'

'Biter still wants to eat you.'

'Meh, one out of two's not bad. That's pretty much one hundred per cent.'

The foxes turned and ran, leaving me and Jess on our own in the dark street.

'That was tense,' she said.

'We had it under control.'

'So, while we wait to hear from The Storm, we go back to our plan for the sanctuary?'

'Starting with Agent Bob.'

# 15

## Ragey Rex

'He'll do it,' Jess said, turning to me from the breakfast bar.

'What does he want?'

'Nothing.'

'Then I'm sorry I called you a rubbish negotiator,' I said.

'You didn't call me a rubbish negotiator.'

'Maybe not out loud.'

Jess gave me some serious stink-eye. 'He and Elle have had an argument and they both need some space, so he's in.'

'This is one of those yesssss! But nooooo! But yesssss! situations,' I said. 'Belle can't break up – they're my favourite fish couple. But equally, Bob can't settle down because he'll lose his edge as an agent.'

'Why's that?'

'Everyone knows that you can't be a great agent if you have people close to you. They're your weakness and that can be exploited.'

'You'd better not spend any more time with Mr Prickles, then.'

'But anyway, I'm glad you're with us on this mission, Bob. And I'm totally rooting for Belle. Yay Belle.'

Jess shook her head. 'When we speak to Miss Fortress tomorrow, we'll get her to ask Dexter about watching the outside of the sanctuary at night.'

'It's called patrolling, Jessticles. We'll get her to tell Dexter to patrol.'

'Whatever.'

'So we're set.'

Getting Bob to school was fine. Mum was used to me taking him out, so she hardly even questioned me about it anymore. I told her that it was because Miss Fortress specialised in fish science and needed to borrow Bob so she could study him, but I'm pretty sure Mum thought he was my version of an imaginary friend. We kind of had this unspoken agreement not to discuss it further, but I overheard her talking to Dad about it at night when she thought I was tucked in bed but I was really sneaking downstairs for a snack.

Anyway, the hard part was getting Bob into the sanctuary and finding a place to hide him where he'd have a good view but Rex and Mrs Fernandes wouldn't see him. The sanctuary was huge, with several rooms inside and a maze of enclosures and pens outside. We needed to be sure that if The Rattler paid a visit, Bob would have the best chance of seeing what he looked like.

I took off my hat and used it to cover Bob's jar until Rex went off to the reptile room. Then we hid Bob's jar in an emptied-out can of meaty chunks with a hole pierced in the side, and hid it behind the other cans, with just enough room for Bob to see out.

We did the rest of our jobs as quietly as possible. We didn't want to draw any attention to ourselves or upset Rex again and risk being fired. When I went to feed Mr Prickles, I saw Dexter perched in a tree. Now that I knew him better, I could see that he did look different from the other pigeons. They all looked unique. He gave me a nod and I knew he'd be watching the sanctuary for us after we left.

'Hey, Mr Prickles,' I said, rubbing him on the soft patch between his ears. 'How are you doing today?'

Mr Prickles closed his eyes and made a purry noise.

'It's so good to see you. Jess and I had a tense evening, yesterday. We were chased by a bunch of foxes.'

Mr Prickles squeaked and rolled himself into a tight, spiky ball.

'It's alright, Mr Prickles, they didn't hurt us and we're hoping they'll lead us to The Storm so we can find out what he knows about The Rattler. I'm sure once we've got more information, we can stop him from coming here and taking your friends.' I picked him up and he unrolled himself so I could tickle him under the chin.

'And my friend, Agent Bob, is concealed in the

kitchen. He's super-smart and really good at spotting things that other people can't, so I'm hoping he'll be able to help us identify The Rattler. And we have another agent patrolling from the air, so we might even be able to find out where The Rattler is taking the animals. Any clue, no matter how small, could help.'

Mr Prickles looked at me and tilted his head to the side. He does that when he's thinking.

'Don't worry,' I said. 'I'll keep you safe, I promise.'

'Alex!' I heard Jess's voice through the bushes. 'Rex wants us to clean out Harry's stable.'

'Of course he does,' I sighed. The donkey and horse areas had the biggest poos, and shovelling poo was as sucky as you'd think.

'Get started and I'll be there in a minute,' Jess called. So bossy.

I put Mr Prickles down by his food and waved goodbye, then I trudged (trudging is the kind of walk you do when you're going somewhere you'd rather not go) over to the stables. Harry was inside spinning round in circles like he'd gone nuts. I kept an eye on his flying hooves while I went to get the poo spade, which is what we had to use for scraping up his dirty bedding. Honestly, you wouldn't think a horse so tiny could make such a mess. Harry was neighing at me as I shovelled up his poo, like he wanted my attention, and when I pulled a stack of clean straw over, he deliberately peed all over it. I threw down the poo spade and stomped to the store barn to get some more.

I opened the door and nearly jumped out of my skin at a movement in the darkness. Rex was sitting on a hay bale, tapping away on a shiny iPhone.

'What are you doing in here?' he said, shoving it in his pocket.

'You wanted me to clean out the horse things,' I said. 'Did you not?'

'Yes. You should be in the stable.'

'I was, but there's not enough straw, so if you want me to do a good job, I need more.' I gestured towards the bale he was sitting on. 'New phone, Rex?'

'Get on with your work,' he said, standing up and storming out of the barn.

First the backpack, then the trainers and now a phone. Where was Rex getting the money to buy all this stuff? And why was he being so secretive about it? There was definitely something going on. I put the information in my agent-brain super-important fact file. I was pretty sure that the time would come when I'd need it.

When I got back to the stable, Jess was talking to Harry. 'Sure, we can try to do that for you when we're here. If you could just keep your eyes and ears open and let us know if you have any information on The Rattler, that would be great.'

'We're doing what for Harry?' I said, dragging the straw behind me. 'Other than cleaning up his giant poos.'

'He wants us to put music on for him when we're here. He likes dancing.'

'Oh, is that what he's trying to do? I thought he was just mad.'

'He says Rex is always in here texting on his phone and that maybe he's up to no good,' Jess said, stroking Harry on his nose. 'But I told him it's probably nothing to worry about. Come on, Alex, we'd better get on with our next jobs before we get into trouble. See you soon, Harry.'

I let Jess walk ahead. 'Harry,' I whispered. 'Watch Rex – try to see what he's texting on his phone. If you get me some good info, I'll play you all the tunes you want.' I winked at him and he laughed, then I followed Jess out of the stable.

Bob and Dexter had nothing to report the next day. It had been a quiet night at the sanctuary and The Rattler hadn't paid a visit. Bob agreed to stay in place for another night, even though the container he was hidden in smelt unpleasant and made him feel nauseous.

In the meantime we got Darth Daver working on a new animalomoly map. He spent his evenings searching the web for strange occurrences that could be related to The Storm, hoping to find some pattern, or a clue to where The Storm might be based. The incidents were happening more and more often. Every day roads were closed because they'd crumbled into underground holes. There were power cuts and blocked drains all over town and nobody dared walk around with their phones out in case they were attacked.

Wherever I was, I felt as though I was being watched.

# 16

## Really Important Person Piper

On the second day, at morning break, Dexter landed on the Reflections Bench next to us. We were looking over the animalomoly map that Dave had brought in. There were hundreds of incident locations marked on it with red dots, and it was becoming clear that the dots formed a rough circle. We were just trying to look at what was in the circle's centre when Jess started to twitch.

'Oh hi, Dexter,' I said. 'Do you have some news?'

'Well done, Dexter,' Jess was saying between twitches. 'That's so helpful. We really appreciate it.'

Dexter nodded and flew off.

'What did he say?' I bounced up and down on the bench.

'The Rattler turned up at the sanctuary last night,' said Jess. 'Dexter couldn't see his face because he was wearing a hood pulled really low and he kept his head down, but when he left, Dexter followed the van.'

'OMG – this is big!' I said. 'Where did the van go?'

'It drove into an underground car park where Dexter couldn't follow, and it didn't come out again, so the car park must be attached to whatever place The Rattler keeps the animals.'

'Did The Rattler steal an animal from the sanctuary?'

'Yes – Dexter heard some of the residents saying it was a rabbit from enclosure 4.'

'Poor guy,' Dave said.

'And where was it?' I asked. 'The underground car park?'

'Greenfields Road East,' said Jess. 'Let's try to find it on the map.'

'There's no need.' Dave put his finger on the map, right in the centre of the red dot circle. 'It's right here.'

'So it *is* all connected.' Jess gazed at the map. 'The Rattler, The Storm, the animalomolies...'

I said a secret "yessssss!" under my breath at Jess's use of my awesome word.

'...They're all part of the same thing. We just need to find out what.'

'We really need to talk to The Storm,' I said. 'Now more than ever.'

Dave had band practice after school that day, so he met me and Jess when we finished at the animal sanctuary, and Mum drove us all to my house. We'd collected Bob from his hiding place in the meat can and we couldn't wait to quiz him on what he'd seen. Mum was a Darth Daver superfan – she thought he was a 'good influence' on me – so she was always annoyingly happy when he came over. She chatted to him constantly, and kept looking at some invisible Dave-shaped thing in the distance after he'd left, saying about twenty times, "Such a lovely boy." It took ages to get her out of the way so we could talk.

We put my laptop on the breakfast bar so we could scan for more animalomolies and try to work out what was lurking in Greenfields Road East.

'Did you find out who The Rattler took last night?' Dave said, while clicking away on the laptop.

'It was Piper.' Jess blinked back a tear. 'She's such a funny rabbit – it's horrible that she's gone.'

'She really liked pranking people,' I said. 'She'd go and poo in the area you just cleaned out and then laugh. And she always hopped over the other rabbits' backs to annoy them. RIP Piper.'

'She's not dead, Alex!' Jess said.

'Oh, is that what that means? I always thought it stood for Really Interesting Person. How does "RIP" mean dead?'

'It stands for Rest In Peace, Double-O-Dumbot.'

'Come to think of it, whenever I've heard people saying it, they're always talking about someone who's died. That totally makes sense now.'

Jess huffed extra loudly.

'The thing is though, Jess. We don't actually know if the animals who've been taken are dead or alive,' I said. 'I know it's terrible to think about, but we have to be prepared for the worst.'

Jess turned to Bob. We'd given him a minute to chill in his tank before we asked him any questions because he was a bit shaken by his experience at the animal sanctuary. He seemed glad to be home, though. I think he and Elle had made up because they were making gooey fishy eyes at each other.

'Did you see anything useful, Bob?' Jess said. 'Did you get a look at The Rattler?'

Dave and I had a Coke-drinking contest while we waited for Jess to do her twitch thing. He won, but then he has a much taller body than I do, so there's a lot more space for the Coke.

'Did he ID the perp?' I asked Jess.

'No.' She looked so disappointed. 'He saw him walking through the centre, but it was really dark and The Rattler kept his hood on the whole time. Bob said it was horrendous, the sound of the keys rattling in the quiet rooms, as The Rattler chose his victim. The animals were too afraid to make a sound in case it caught his attention, so there was just silence, and footsteps, and the keys. Bob was afraid he'd be discovered and taken himself.'

'So didn't he find out anything useful?' I said.

Jess gave me a look and Dave nudged me gently.

'I mean, I'm really sorry, Bob – that does sound super-creepy. I'm glad you're OK.' I gave him a thumbs-up and a smile. 'But didn't you find out anything useful?'

Jess juddered about again and smiled. 'Good for Piper.'

'What?' I said.

'She bit The Rattler when he was carrying her out.'

I smiled too. 'RIP Piper.'

Jess rolled her eyes. 'But Bob went to all that trouble and we still don't know who The Rattler is.'

'And we haven't managed to get a meeting with The Storm,' I said.

'We're messing up the case,' said Jess.

'Speak for yourself, Jessticles – I'm doing an epic job.'

'How do you work that out?'

'I got Rex and his mum out of the sanctuary so we could snoop.'

'By letting a snake out of a tank.'

'I got the photos of the log book on my phone,' I said.

'And then you let squirrels steal it from you.'

'Well, I found out that Taran was lying.'

'About being a vegan.' Jess rubbed her face with her hands like I was making her tired or something.

'Come on, guys, don't argue,' Dave said. 'Let's do something productive, like trying to find out what's on Greenfields Road East. I've downloaded a list of all the buildings and businesses on the street for us to look through.'

'Wow – you did all that? I'm definitely going back to calling you Cybershadow.' It was so cool having a hacker on the team.

Me and Jess stood behind Dave and looked over his shoulder at the screen.

'The buildings on the road are all really big – it's like an industrial estate,' said Dave.

'So The Rattler can't have been going back to his house, then?' I said.

'No, I wouldn't have thought so. And I've found what looks like the underground car park on the map. It connects to these three buildings.' Dave pointed at some shapes on the map.

'So let's focus on those first,' Jess said. 'Can we find out what the buildings are?'

'One step ahead of you, Jess,' said Dave.

I sniggered. 'You just got burned by Dave. He never burns anyone.'

'Shut up, Alex.' Jess whacked me on the arm.

'So this building is a bunch of offices and a warehouse for a company that makes wheelie bins,' Dave said. 'And this really big one is a recycling plant – they collect paper waste from companies in the area and shred it, then recycle it.'

'So far, so boring,' I said. 'What about the smaller building?'

'That's the strange thing,' said Dave. 'The third building doesn't have a business listed for it. There's no description, no information, nothing.'

'How very mysterious,' I said, doing my wiggly mysterious fingers. 'That has evil villain hideout written all over it. Isn't there some way of finding out who owns it?'

'One step ahead of you, Alex,' Dave said.

'Would you like some ice for that burn, Alex?' Jess smirked.

'There's this thing called Land Registry and it tells you who owns buildings and land in the

UK.' Dave opened another window on his browser.

'How did you even know that?' I said.

Dave looked up for a moment. 'Google.'

'Sorry,' I said. 'Rookie question.'

'It costs £3 to run a search, but I bypassed that because this is an emergency, and the result should come through any time...'

A page of information flicked onto the screen.

'...now.' Dave rolled back his shoulders in this really awesome way that made him look like a boss.

We stared at the computer screen. Finally – a good, solid clue.

'I can't believe it,' Jess said.

'Yep, didn't see that coming.' I read the words in front of me, and then read them again and again to be sure. But it was there in black and white: the building belonged to SPARC Industries.

'This can't be good,' said Jess. 'I wonder what they're up to in there?'

'And how are the animals involved?' Dave turned on his stool to face us.

'We need to get inside,' I said.

'That's impossible!' Jess frowned. 'Greenfields

Road East is on the other side of town, so there's no way we can get there on our own. And even if we got there, how would we get in to look around?'

'Do you know what I love, more than anything else in the world, except Mr Prickles?' I said.

'I'm sure you're going to tell us.'

'Well, seeing as you want to know so badly, I'll tell you. I love an impossible mission: skill level nine thousand; chances of success slim to none.'

Dave smiled. 'So you think it can be done?'

'Of course it can be done, my tall, dark friend,' I said. 'I'm already formulating an amazing plan.'

'Don't tell me,' Jess said. 'All you need is a shoelace, a laser watch and a tank of piranhas.'

'Wrong!' I said. 'All I need is Miss Fortress.' I thought for a second. 'But the laser watch and tank of piranhas could be useful, too.'

# 17

## Miss F is Back in the Game

'Two words for you, Miss…' I said. 'Montgomery McMonaghan.'

Miss Fortress spat her coffee all over her desk, me, and Jess. 'What?'

'He's involved in the animal disappearances,' said Jess. 'And they're connected to the…'

'Animalomolies,' I said.

'The what?' Miss Fortress wiped coffee of some papers with her sleeve.

'The power cuts, the blocked drains, the

squirrel muggings, the howling foxes, the dog attacks, the collapsing roads, the house fires… I could go on,' I said with the air of a highly trained professional expert.

'I should have known!' She looked at her coffee-soaked cardigan, took it off and stuffed it in a drawer.

I knew this would get her attention.

'So will you help?' I said.

'Of course, I'll do whatever I can to stop that monster,' she said.

'Except actually show your face anywhere near him in case he recognises you, you mean,' said Jess, with typical Jess rudeness.

Miss Fortress gave her a hard look. 'Yes, except that. I'm not being selfish, you know, Jess – it's for…'

'The greater good. Yeah, yeah, you've told us before.' Jess did one of her most vicious eye rolls yet.

'Ooh – I've just realised something!' I said, feeling very excited and rather smug.

'What is it?' said Jess. 'Have you worked out who The Rattler is?'

'No, but I've worked out that Miss Fortress is a

Ravenclaw, and you, Jessticles, are a classic Gryffindor. This is why you disagree so much.'

'Brilliant,' Jess said in her most sarcastic voice, although I could tell she was secretly pleased about being a Gryffindor. 'And is there a Hogwarts house that explains why you're the way you are?'

'I'm glad you asked,' I said. 'I'm actually a unique combination of all the best qualities from all four houses. I'm a SlytherGriffPuffyClaw.'

'Of course you are.'

'Can we get back to business, please?' Miss Fortress said.

'Hang on,' said Jess. 'You've ignored us for weeks and now that your old boyfriend's involved, you're suddenly interested again and think you can start bossing us around?'

'Yes, that's exactly right. I'm the grown-up here,' said Miss Fortress. 'And I haven't been ignoring you, I've been working on something that I thought might help you both with the investigation. It's taken up all of my work time, and my evenings, too, not that you'll be grateful.'

'Is it a stealth jet?' I said.

'No.'

'A freeze ray?'

'Of course not.'

'A genetically mutated chupacabra with X-ray eyes?'

'Shut up, Alex!' Jess snapped. 'What is it, Miss? And please give us the short, understandable answer, not the over-complicated science one.'

Miss Fortress looked disappointed. 'It's a device that determines the exact frequency of your neurological output and tunes into the transmissions…'

'Can I stop you there?' I said. 'You're doing the fancy blah blah blahs again. Keep it simple Prof.'

'Short. Understandable. Answer,' said Jess.

'It's a device that might allow you and Jess to combine powers for a few moments.'

Jess's eyebrows shot towards the ceiling and I jumped off my chair.

'So I'll be able to understand animals?' I said. 'And Jess will know if people are lying?'

'Not exactly,' Miss Fortress's hair started coming loose from her bun thing and flapping around by her ears. It made it look like her head had wings. This always happened when she got excited. 'You'd still have to work together – you'd need to be connected. And while you were, you would be able to feel the effect of each other's power.'

'I can't get my head round this – that's insane!' I said.

'So if we asked an animal questions, we'd both be able to hear the answers and know if the animal was telling the truth?' said Jess.

'In theory, yes.'

Jess rolled her eyes. 'I knew there would be a catch.'

'There's no catch. Just that it's untested, highly dangerous and likely to cause brain damage.'

'I like those odds!' I said. I was so excited to try this max-boost power-combo thing. It sounded awesome.

'And it's not ready yet,' said Miss Fortress. 'But it will be soon.'

'While you're busy with your new exciting way to cause us pain and embarrassment,' Jess said, 'there's something else we need you to do.'

'We need you to organise a Year 6 school trip,' I said. 'One that will get us out of school, away from our parents and close to the SPARC facility for a day.'

Miss Fortress looked at the map of Greenfields

Road East. 'What about the recycling plant? The head is always banging on about being environmentally friendly so she'd probably go for it. And I could make it seem educational. In my annoying sciencey way.' She gave us a stink-eye.

'Perfect!' I said. 'How soon can we go? FYI, it needs to be really soon.'

'I'm supposed to visit in advance and carry out a risk assessment,' said Miss Fortress. 'But I can just make that up. No one cares about all that health and safety nonsense anyway. Then I have to get it signed off and get a letter out to parents.'

'So how long?' said Jess.

'A week.'

'We can work with that,' I said, the seed of a plan sprouting in my mind. 'Can you please do something for us right now? We're only going to get one shot at this, so I want to do a reccy of the location before we go on the trip.'

'What do you need?'

It was one of those big hero moments. If it was in a movie, there would be a dramatic pause where all the other characters looked at me with awe and respect. I was the leader – the man with the plan. They were counting on me.

I took a breath and gave them my best Nick Fury look of authority and bad-A-ness. 'I need a note for my mum.'

The next day was Saturday. Before our shift at the sanctuary, we got in my mum's car and drove across town to Greenfield Road East. Miss Fortress had told my mum that we'd volunteered to take some pictures of the recycling plant for our school display. But she was still suspicious until we told her that Dave was coming too.

'Such a lovely boy,' she smiled, and took her car keys off the hook in the hall.

When we got to Greenfield Road East, Mum pulled the car over.

'Thanks, Mrs Sparrow,' Jess said, clicking off her seatbelt. Up until about a month ago, she'd still had to use a booster seat – it was hilarious. 'We won't be too long.'

'That's fine, I have my John Grisham to read.' Mum pulled a book out of her handbag. 'And I'll be able to see you the whole time. Have fun, kids.'

We closed the car doors and walked up Greenfield Road East towards the recycling plant and evil SPARC secret base. It was really cold, so we didn't look out of place with our hoods on and our scarves pulled up to cover half of our faces. It was unlikely that anyone from SPARC would recognise us, but there was no harm in being careful. Also, it made it feel more undercover-y, so the whole thing was a bit more exciting.

'It looks like there have been loads of holes in this road,' Dave said, staring down at the ground which was covered with circles of fresh tarmac where the road had been repaired.

'It must have been a priority target. Look.' Jess pointed at the branches of a nearby tree that had been covered with little spikes.

'OMG, it's like an armoured tree monster! They must be planning to bring the trees to life so they can rampage through the city, destroying everything in their paths.'

Dave laughed.

'People put those spikes up to stop birds from nesting on the branches,' Jess said. 'Or squirrels, maybe.'

'I knew that,' I said.

'Whatever, stinker,' Jess rolled her eyes. 'By the way, you know trees are already alive, right?'

'If this area's been targeted by the animals, isn't

it a bit weird that there aren't reporters here like there are all over town?' I said.

'Yeah, that is strange,' said Dave. 'Maybe the holes have been fixed and the incidents haven't been reported.'

'Like they're trying to keep the press away.' Jess shivered.

As we walked up the road, I couldn't shake the feeling that we weren't alone. On the left side of the street were the buildings – all large and with grassy bits around them. On the right side of the road was a chain link fence, and beyond it just open, scraggy grassland covered in weeds and shrubs and piles of dirt. It looked like it had been cleared to make space for more buildings, but they hadn't started doing the work yet.

'I feel like someone's watching us,' I said.

'She's called your mum.' Jess's rude tone was hearable, even through her woolly scarf.

'Not Mum. Someone else.'

'We're coming up to the SPARC building,' Dave whispered. 'Let's get some photos and get out of here as fast as we can.'

The SPARC building was the only one on the street that didn't have a sign. There was nothing on it that gave an idea of what it was or who owned it. It was a grey cement block, with those one-way windows that you couldn't see in through. It wasn't nice to think that someone could be watching us from inside and we wouldn't even know about it. The ledges of the windows and the roof were covered in those anti-bird spikes. Overall it didn't look very inviting.

'I don't think they like having visitors,' I said.

'Look at all the CCTV cameras,' said Jess. There were cameras stuck all around the building, so there's no way anyone could get in or out without being seen.

'What about the underground car park?' I said. 'Maybe we could sneak in that way?'

But the entrance to the underground car park was also surrounded by cameras and had some kind of high-tech security entry system.

'We'll take some pictures and figure it out when we get home.' Dave was always so calm.

'K, but we'll have to make it look like we're taking selfies and not photographing the evil lair.'

Jess dug her phone out of her pocket and held it up in front of us.

'Silly faces,' I said. 'To make it look authentic.'

We stuck out our tongues and made bunny ears while Jess snapped away at the building and car park. She focused on the front door of the SPARC lair, which was made of darkened glass. 'I have no idea how we're going to get in.'

A side door at the recycling plant next to SPARC opened, and a man and a woman wearing hi-vis jackets came out, wheeling a tall, plastic box on a trolley. They walked a few metres down the path and then towards the main entrance of SPARC.

'That's it, Jessticles,' I said. 'That's how we're getting in.'

'They probably have ID checks though – we need to know what the security's like. But if either of us go in now, they'll recognise us when we…'

'Infiltrate for realz,' I said.

'Wait here, guys, I'll just be a sec,' Dave said. And before we could stop him, he ran up to the entrance and followed the recycling people through the double doors.

'Do you think he's going to fight his way past the armed guards and hack their computer system to give us top-level clearance?' I said.

'Probably not.' Jess snorted, and white puffs came out of her nose like a dragon.

'Good, because Mum would be a rubbish getaway driver.'

Two minutes later, I was relieved-slash-a bit disappointed to see Dave walk out of the building without any signs of a struggle.

'I know what you have to do to get through security,' he said. 'But I'm going to need a bit of time to make you some fake IDs, and you'll need to think up a cunning plan,' he winked at me. 'Let's get back to the car.'

We turned and moved back towards the car, the feeling that we were being watched growing with every step we took, so much that I was actually relieved to get back to Mum. Don't tell anyone that, though.

After she'd dropped Dave home, Mum left me and Jess at the animal sanctuary for our shift. Our plan was coming together and the atmosphere at the sanctuary was a bit more chill than it had been. When Piper was abducted, everyone was really upset, but it also gave the other animals some breathing space. They felt like they were safe, for a while at least. Rex still had serious beef with me, but not enough to do anything about it. He did his jobs and we did ours, and I got a bit of time to hang out with Mr Prickles and fill him in on everything that had been going on.

What me and Jess didn't know then was that we'd reached the beginning of the end.

# 18

## Hostile Negotiations

After a long shift at the sanctuary, feeding unidentifiable food items to a bunch of hungry animals, cleaning up after them, encouraging them to exercise and breaking up fights (the swan was always causing trouble), Jess and I closed the gate behind us and started walking towards my house.

'So we have five days until the school trip,' Jess said.

'Five days to come up with a brilliant plan.' I had the startings of one, but… 'There are so many things we still don't know. I'd feel better if we had answers to some of our questions. We're only going to get one opportunity to infiltrate SPARC.'

'You think we're out of our depth?'

'Completely,' I said. 'But that's not going to stop us. We'll be the underdogs and everyone knows the underdog always wins.'

We turned down Oak Avenue. It wasn't half as creepy in the daylight.

'Nice to not be running away from foxes,' said Jess.

'I don't know. It was kind of fun in a scary way.'

We were halfway down the road when General Pow and Biter appeared from one of the gardens in front of us.

'Not so fun I want to do it again right now, though,' I said, bracing myself for a sprint.

'I don't think they're here to chase us,' Jess said as we got close.

'Then what?'

Jess spasmed for a few seconds while Biter licked her lips at me. It made me feel very uncomfortable.

'I think Biter's got a thing for me,' I said.

'If you mean she wants to bite you, then you're absolutely right.'

'What did they say?'

'They had a message for us from The Storm. He said, as he cannot keep us away, he has no choice but to deal with us himself. Therefore he will parley with us.'

'OMG, an actual, real-life parley,' I said. 'OK. It needs to be at a time of our choosing and on neutral ground.'

General Pow growled and took a step closer to us, then turned and nodded at Biter. Biter started making this horrible hacking cough noise until something flew from her mouth and landed at Jess's feet, covered in drool.

'Er, what the heck is that?' I peered down at it, not wanting to get too close. 'It looks like a bit of chewed-up plastic.'

'There's something on it.' Jess crouched down for a better look. 'Words, I think, and a pattern – circles and lines, and ... oh my God.'

'What?'

'It's a piece of a travel mug. One that says 'Science Is Sexy' and has molecules all over it.'

'But the only person who has that mug is Miss Fortress,' I gasped and glared at General Pow. 'What have you done to her?'

Biter made a noise that really sounded like she was laughing.

Jess, who had gone even paler than her usual shade of ghost white, started to twitch.

'General Pow said now that they have something we want, they will make the terms. If we don't agree, or if we try to deceive them in any way, we'll never see Miss Fortress again.'

'Oh bums,' I said. I couldn't see that there was anything we could do except agree and try to get back on their good side. 'What are their terms?'

'Monday, at sunset. Rendezvous on the school field.'

'Sunset. Totally cool time to have a parley.'

'And there's one more thing,' Jess said. 'We need to prove that we aren't his enemy, or he will finish us.'

'A no-pressure sunset parley. This. Is. Awesome.'

General Pow turned and started walking away. Biter grinned at us and spat something else on the ground, then ran to catch up with the General.

'What is that?' Jess said. 'It doesn't look like the cup.'

I bent down and picked it up by one end. My stomach lurched when I realised what I had in my hand: wet, broken and with splashes of blood on it. 'It's a pigeon feather.'

'Oh God,' Jess whispered. 'Dexter.'

'He probably tried to fight them off when they took Miss Fortress. If they did take her.'

'Surely someone would have reported her missing, though?'

'I don't know, Jess. And we have no way of finding out. We don't know where she lives, or if she has any friends or family.'

'I think she mentioned once that her family is back in Singapore.' Jess rubbed her face, leaving pink marks on her cheeks.

'So she's alone here,' I said, thinking for the first time about how hard it must have been for Miss Fortress to give up her life and identity for the sake of others.

'We don't even know her real name,' said Jess. 'I don't think we ever bothered to ask her.'

'Poor Miss Fortress,' I sighed. 'But she must be alive, or The Storm wouldn't have anything to bargain with.'

'And what about Dexter?' said Jess.

We looked at each other, but neither of us could bring ourselves to talk about what might have happened to him.

'We'd better get back to yours and come up with that plan,' said Jess.

We got straight to work. The only idea we had for where Miss Fortress was being held was the SPARC building, so the best use of our time was to gather as much information as possible and think up a way into SPARC. Information meant power, and with it we might be able to negotiate for Miss Fortress's release. We hoped we'd be able to get Dexter back, too. We printed the photos of the SPARC building and spread them along the breakfast bar. We used a red Sharpie to circle all the cameras and potential entrances. It was clear we'd have no chance of sneaking in undetected, so we were going to have to trick our way in. Luckily, this type of espionage was something I excelled in.

'We should probably stream the local news, just in case there have been any developments in the animalomolies,' Jess said.

'Good thinking.' I set up the browser window. 'Keep an eye on it for us, would you, Bob?'

'So what are you thinking?' said Jess. 'I'm guessing it has something to do with the recycling plant.'

'We disguise ourselves as plant workers, take one of those wheelie trolleys and a collection box, and walk straight through the front door,' I said.

'Are they really going to believe we work there, though? Neither of us looks particularly old.'

'We'll wear fake moustaches,' I said.

'I don't think that's going to be convincing enough.'

'Beards then. You'll look like a leprechaun.'

'We could say we're on work experience there, I suppose,' said Jess. 'And when we have Dave's fake IDs, we might just get away with it.'

'Yeah, I bet Dave can make them look legit!'

'And once we're through the front door, what then? When Dave followed those other plant workers in, he said they had to empty their pockets and get patted down before they were allowed in.'

'Good old Dave,' I said. 'It was quick thinking of him to go in and say he was looking for his dad.'

'So we can't have anything incriminating in our pockets, and we still need to find out where exactly in the building they keep the animals.'

'We might just have to wing it,' I said.

'Hold on a sec,' said Jess. 'Bob's trying to say

something.' She twitched for a moment. 'He wants us to turn up the volume on the laptop.'

I leant over the laptop and turned the sound up to full. There was a news report on, about a badger attacking a dog walker and breaking his leg. The reporter was asking our resident animal expert, a.k.a. Taran, to explain why the badger would have acted in such a way.

'Urgh. Nugget-scoffing Taran,' I said.

'Shush, Bob's trying to concentrate.' Jess twitched. 'Pause it,' she said.

'Why?'

'Just do it – Bob's on to something.'

I reached over and paused the stream. It froze on an image of Taran, looking into the camera with a smile that said he was the most trustworthy person in the world. Jess shuddered away at Bob's tank.

'What does he want?' I said.

'He recognises Taran's voice.'

'From the TV?'

'No, from his time at the sanctuary. Do you remember when Piper was taken? Piper bit The Rattler, and Bob remembers The Rattler saying lots of bad swears. When he heard Taran's voice on the news just now, he thought it sounded similar to The Rattler's.'

'OK, OK, I'm getting excited,' I said. 'But it isn't solid proof – we know Bob hears things wrong through the water sometimes.'

'He doesn't always hear things that well,' said Jess, 'but he's the best person we know at noticing little things that other people might miss.'

'So what has he noticed?' I said, bouncing up and down on my stool.

'Look at Taran's hand,' said Jess, and she pointed to the screen.

'What is that?' I peered at a mark on Taran's right hand. It was red and scabby. 'It looks like a cut.'

'What it looks like,' said Jess, 'is a bite. A rabbit bite.'

I gasped. 'Piper!'

'Piper,' Jess nodded.

'Then it's him! I knew it! Taran is The Rattler.'

'Oh God, I think he is.' Jess rubbed her face with her hands. 'I'm so sorry. I've been such an idiot.'

This was very not-Jess behaviour, and I thought for a second that she was tricking me.

'Um, what?'

'I could have spoken to Meena, when we met Taran right at the start of all this. She wanted to tell me something but I didn't want to embarrass myself in front of him.'

'Don't be too hard on yourself. He does have delicious eyes and cool clothes and this charismatic way about him.'

'You suspected him, though.'

'A bit, but a lot of that was just because it annoyed me that you changed around him. I knew he'd told a lie, but I didn't honestly think he was The Rattler. That son of a biscuit.'

'Alex, this is your perfect opportunity to rub my face in the mess I made. Why aren't you doing it?'

I looked at Jess. When I was having a hard time earlier in the year, she was the only person who'd given me a break. And although I don't like to talk about it, I'm well aware that I made a few mistakes back then. Jess knew when to be hard on me, and when to be kind, and that was what made her a good friend. I wanted to be the same to her.

'We got to the truth eventually,' I said. 'That's what matters.'

'Maybe we can use this,' Jess pulled a photo of the SPARC building towards her, 'to make our plan less totally likely to fail.'

'And we have solid information that we can trade for Miss Fortress's release,' I said.

'We can do this. We just need to come up with a plan.'

'Aw, Jessticles, I'm proud of you,' I said, giving her a squeeze. 'So proud that I feel a sick rap coming on.'

Jess banged her head down on the counter. 'End me now.'

# 19

## We Parley Like it's Friday Night

We spent the weekend trying not to worry. We heard nothing from Miss Fortress and we didn't see Dexter. I was actually looking forward to going to school on Monday because part of me hoped I'd walk into the classroom and Miss Fortress would be there, drinking her coffee and snapping at everyone like usual. But when we went into class, it was Miss Hussein taking the register. It was strange to be greeted with a smile instead of tutting and yawning. Although now I understood why Miss Fortress was the way she was, I kind of got why she was always tired and stressed. And all Miss Hussein could tell us was that Miss Fortress wasn't going to be in school that day.

We went to the sanctuary after school. It was hard to concentrate on my jobs because all I could think about was our meeting with The Storm. A good agent knows that you should never underestimate your enemy, and even though The Storm was an animal, I had nothing but respect for him. Over the past month, he'd chipped away at the infrastructure of our town. He'd attacked us where it hurt, targeting our power, transport systems and technology. He'd kidnapped our mentor. Also, he was called The Storm, so he was clearly an epic bad-A.

At the time we usually finished work, we left through the front door as usual but then snuck down the side of the building to the garden, keeping a lookout for Rex. When the coast was clear, me and Jess ran down the garden, staying close to the fence. It was almost too easy. When we were halfway down, I grabbed Jess and flung us both into a huge bush.

'What did you do that for?' Jess whispered. 'Rex is across the other side, near the house. There's no way he can see us from there.'

'Just trying to liven things up,' I said.

'Idiot,' Jess huffed, brushing bits of leaf and twig off her clothes. Without waiting for me to get up, she ran towards the end of the garden. I laughed to myself as I followed.

The furthest boundary of the animal sanctuary backed on to the school field. As we wouldn't be able to get into the school grounds through the main gate without being seen, the back fence was our best shot. Unfortunately, that meant either burrowing or climbing.

'So how are we going to do this?' I said, assessing the fence with my super-agent vision. 'If only we had some sticky toffee, the leaves from a palm tree and a jet pack.'

'Or a broken fence panel,' Jess said, sliding one of the wooden planks back. 'Rex and his mum keep fixing it, but someone always breaks it again. I think it must be The Storm trying to get access to the sanctuary.'

The sun was going down, and the warmth and light of the day was fading fast. I eyed the hole in the fence, which wasn't especially big and wondered if I'd be able to squeeze through.

'After you, tubs,' Jess said. 'If you get stuck, I'll give you a push.'

To climb or to squeeze? That was the question.

'We can't be late for The Storm,' Jess said, tapping her foot in a really annoying way. It was alright for her – she was the size of a meerkat.

'Did you bring the emergency butter?' I said.

'We don't have emergency butter. Just get yourself through that hole. If your giant head fits, the rest of you will squish through fine.'

I sucked my gut in as hard as I could, leant back, and swung through, hoping that if I had some momentum behind me, it might just propel me into the field. I'd like to tell you that was how it happened, but unfortunately there was a bit of shoving involved. At one point Jess accidentally touched my bottom. I'm not proud of it and I never want to speak of it again.

'Right,' I said, dusting myself down. 'On with the mission!'

We were in the far corner of the field, behind the vegetable patch where we'd found Boris and Noodle, and where we'd spotted the animal meeting that morning after our argument. It was strange being in the school grounds at this time. Even though it wasn't that late, it was so quiet and the light was so dim that it felt like another world.

'We need some background music,' I said. 'Lay me down a phat beat, MC J-Law.'

'We don't need background music. We're breaking and entering – we need to keep quiet.'

'Ooh, breaking and entering, I like the sound of that. That's real jail-time stuff. Although technically the fence was already broken, so it was more sliding and entering. Is sliding and entering a thing?'

'I'm pretty sure it will be if we get caught.' Jess looked around.

The lights were on in the school building, but that was way off. The only things in our corner of the field were some trees and bushes, the vegetable patch and a rusty old shed.

'Agent Alex and Sideshow Jess are locked up in a maximum-security facility for sliding and entering the forbidden vegetable garden in the dead of night.'

'Alex, it's 5pm.'

'Same thing.'

'It is literally not the same thing.'

A low growl came from some bushes just in front of us, and General Pow stepped into our path, followed by Biter.

Jess jerked for a couple of seconds. 'General Pow said The Storm will see us now. We must follow him.'

'Got to love an escort,' I said. 'I feel like we're being taken to see Aslan or something. Oh, fudge – is The Storm a lion? Is he? Is he?'

'I seriously doubt it,' Jess said, as we followed the two foxes towards the shed. As we got closer, all sorts of animals emerged from the undergrowth and stood watching us, like security guards. There were loads of foxes, dogs and badgers – some of them were really big and lots of them were growling. It was quite intimidating. The door to the shed swung open and General Pow and Biter stopped and stood at either side of the gaping black entrance.

'The Storm is inside,' said Jess. 'We're to go in slowly with our hands where they can see them.'

'Please be a lion,' I whispered, as we walked through the door. 'Please be a lion, please be a lion.'

'Shut up, Alex,' Jess said. 'And remember to be respectful.'

The door closed behind us and we were left standing in the pitch black, with only the sound of the wind creaking through the shed.

'Mr The Storm, your majesty,' I said in my politest voice. 'May we please have a light? Our pathetic human eyes cannot penetrate the darkness as yours can, oh great one.'

I heard Jess sigh next to me, then something brushed past my leg. I tried not to scream like a girl. I pictured a lion the size of a horse circling us in the darkness, deciding which one of us to eat first. It wasn't the way I'd planned on dying, but if I was going out, I'd go out like a hero.

'If you're hungry, Sir Storm, I'll be a much tastier meal. I mean, look at Jess – she only eats vegetables so she'd be too crunchy. You'd be picking bits of her out of your teeth for days.'

There was a click, and a flicker, and the room was flooded with light. Well, I say flooded but it was a rubbish light and a dark cloth had been put over it to make it dimmer, so it was more trickled than flooded. The room was trickled with light. I blinked a couple of times, trying to get used to the faint glow and looked around me for The Storm.

'Where is he, Jess?' I said. 'Did he leave?'

Jess elbowed me and nodded towards the back of the shed. 'He's right in front of you.'

I lowered my gaze to see a group of animals sitting on the floor. There was a beaten-up looking brown rabbit with a torn ear, a knobbly toad, and between them, there was…

'Colin!' I said. 'What are you doing here? Mrs Bushall next door has been looking for you for ages.'

'Alex,' Jess gave me a look.

'Jess, it's Colin, the cat from next door,' I said. 'When we've finished speaking to The Storm, I'll take you home if you like, Colin? We could snuggle you into my backpack.'

'Alex,' Jess whacked me, 'that's The Storm.'

'*What*?' I looked at Colin and he looked at me. It was definitely the fat grey cat I'd chased out of my garden a bunch of times. Which, come to think of it, probably hadn't given him the best first impression of me. Or second or third impression. 'Well, this is awkward.'

Jess started to twitch, and I stood by patiently (impatiently) waiting to hear what he had to say.

'His name is Cumulus Maximus,' Jess said. 'But we may call him The Storm.'

'Good choice,' I said, giving him a thumbs-up. 'Way cooler than Colin.'

'And he demands to know why we continue to plague him in his quest. Our constant interference and asking of questions is tiresome to him. He has witnessed us moving freely through enemy territory and fraternising with those who seek to destroy him. The only conclusion he can draw is that we are in league with those who have incited war against his kind.'

'We're not trying to plague you,' I said. 'We're not your enemy. But the attacks on people don't seem right. And you've kidnapped two of our people. Where are Miss Fortress and Dexter?'

The Storm tilted his ears back and hissed at me, then meowed at General Pow, who was standing behind us.

'The Storm says that what isn't right is humans treating animals as though they have no right to life. The culling, the experimenting, the abuse – it has to stop. And if going to war is the only way for him to achieve his objective, then so be it.'

Jess knelt down on the floor and looked at The

Storm. 'You're absolutely right,' she said. 'The way some humans treat animals is disgusting, and I don't blame you for being angry.'

'But it isn't all of us,' I said. 'In the same way that some animals are great and others are total jerks. I'm not going to lie – there are some really bad people in this world. But there are good ones too. And the best way to fight the bad is for all the good guys to join together and stand up for what is right. Will you return our friends? I'm not saying that you and me are ever going to be best mates, but that doesn't mean we can't help each other.'

The Storm tilted his head slightly, as though he was thinking about what we'd said.

'Oh, Alex and Jess. You took your time,' an irritated voice came from the doorway.

We spun around to see Miss Fortress. She had a few scratches on her, her hair was a mess and she looked like she'd got dressed in the dark. So basically she looked the same as usual. It was a relief.

'Should we hug?' I said. 'I feel like we should hug.'

'We should not,' Miss Fortress snapped, as Jess

gasped in horror. 'I've been stuck in this shed for two ghastly days, being guarded by vicious animals and given scraps foraged from rubbish bins to eat. I'm in no mood to hug.'

'Good to see you, too,' I said.

'Thank you for returning Miss Fortress,' Jess said to The Storm. 'But where is our other friend – Dexter?'

Biter barked and Jess juddered.

'But shouldn't animals and birds be on the same side?' Jess said. 'He was no threat.'

'What?' Me and Miss Fortress asked at the same time.

'They don't know where he is or if he's OK. He tried to protect Miss Fortress and was injured. The foxes left him unconscious in the car park.'

'Well then, I don't see why we should help them,' Miss Fortress shouted.

Jess had gone pink with anger and Miss Fortress was shouting very unteachery swears at the animals around us who were snarling back. Our negotiations were falling apart. I closed my eyes for a moment, trying to think. What was the best way forward?

'This isn't helping!' I shouted. The shed went

silent. 'We all want the same thing and the only way we're going to get it is if we work together.' I turned to The Storm. 'You must have some good trackers in your unit. Can you send some of them to look for our friend as a gesture of goodwill?'

The Storm nodded and I heard the scurry of paws on the frozen ground outside.

'Can I ask what happened to you, The Storm?' Jess said. 'It's clear that you've been wronged somehow and we'd like to help put it right, if we can.'

He stood up and started slowly pacing back and forth across the shed, speaking in a mixture of low rumbles and growls.

'What's he saying, Jess?'

'He was abducted from his home by the one they call The Rattler...'

'The Rattler!' I gasped. 'We know him! We hate him!'

'He was imprisoned in a laboratory where he was subjected to weeks of torture. Horrors took place of which he would rather not speak.'

'He must mean the SPARC building! That's what's in there – an evil laboratory!'

'There were many others: comrades and

friends – honourable souls who did not deserve the fates that befell them.'

'Why are you talking funny?' I said to Jess.

'I'm not talking funny. I'm repeating what the Storm is saying.'

'So he talks funny?'

'You know he can hear you, right?'

Jess, The Storm and his two henchmen all gave me a look.

'I just want to know what it sounds like so I can be part of the moment,' I said. 'Do it in his voice.'

'But he's Scottish, and his voice is really low. He says The Storm like "The Stor-um".'

'Awesome.'

Jess twitched again. 'The experiments caused him immense physical pain and emotional anguish, but they also transformed him in a way The Rattler did not foresee. As a result of the tests, he became exponentially smarter.'

'I thought you said he was Scottish?'

'He is.'

'You sound Indian.'

'I have something that might help,' Miss Fortress butted in.

Jess turned to The Storm. 'Will you excuse us for one minute?'

We turned to Miss F. 'What is it?' I said.

'The device we were discussing that might allow you to share in each other's powers. I finished it. It's in my pocket.'

'Is it safe?' Jess said, wrinkling her nose.

'Safe or not, we are doing this!' Oh yes, this was happening.

'It probably won't kill you,' Miss Fortress shrugged.

Jess sighed. 'The Storm, if you don't mind, Miss Fortress needs to give us something from her pocket. It will help my friend to understand our conversation.'

The Storm nodded, so Miss F felt in the pocket of her coat and pulled out the gadget. When The Storm saw it, he hissed. I guess it looked similar to something he'd been tortured with at the lab. The animals all jumped up, backs arching and teeth bared.

'No, no! This is for us,' Jess said, pointing at herself and me. 'We won't put it near you.'

It was clear The Storm didn't believe her. The animals formed a circle around us and moved in.

This negotiation business was so much harder than I thought.

But then a streak of orange slithered into the circle and hissed. It was the corn snake from the animal sanctuary.

'He's telling The Storm to give us a chance,' Jess said.

'Oh, lucky I set him free then, isn't it, Jessticles?'

'Shut up, Alex, I'm trying to listen.' She twitched for a moment. 'The Storm says we may continue.'

We attached the suction pads behind our ears like Miss Fortress had shown us, then we held hands. I was excited about finally being able to hear what Jess hears when she speaks to animals, but I was scared, too, because if I knew Miss Fortress, which I did, then it was probably going to hurt.

The animals looked on suspiciously.

'Ready?' Jess said.

'Let's do it.'

Together, we flipped the switches on the device.

There was a moment when nothing happened and then an electric charge stabbed through the suction pad into the side of my head like a knife.

'Son of a biscuit!' I shouted, clutching my hands to my temples and bending over double, like that was going to make a difference.

Jess didn't swear but she bit her lip so hard it bled and almost broke my hand because she was squeezing it so hard.

The pain continued for one, two, three seconds, and then finally sputtered out.

'Do you feel any different?' Jess said.

'Well, my head hurts a whole lot more than it did a minute ago. But other than that, I don't think so.'

The Storm, the toad and the rabbit looked at us like the scientists first look at the dinosaurs when they walk into Jurassic Park.

'Will you tell us more about your experiences at the lab, Your Royal Stormness?' I said, and I focused every bit of my concentration and energy on him.

Jess twitched away, but for me? Nothing.

'Are you getting any of this?' Jess said.

'It didn't flipping work!' I ripped the suction pad off my face. 'All that pain for nothing!'

'I guess it was worth a try,' Miss Fortress said, snatching the gadget back without looking the slightest bit worried that she'd almost made our brains bleed.

'Was it though?' Jess huffed at her.

Jess went into full-on judders and, as usual, all I could do was stand next to her, waiting to find out what was going on.

'The Storm is impressed that we would go to such lengths in pursuit of our goal. His enemy's enemy is his friend, so he's willing to ally himself with us. He wants to hear our plan.'

# 20

## Nothing but Darkness

When the meeting with The Storm was over, we walked Miss Fortress back to her car. She was really peed off, but her worry for Dexter was bigger than her anger, so she didn't talk much. The Storm had promised to return him to us if his trackers were successful.

Miss Fortress was back in school the next day and we focused on our plan to infiltrate SPARC. With the help of The Storm's army, it all seemed much more doable. I felt optimistic. Until we got to the sanctuary after school and it was clear that something bad had happened. The animals were upset. As soon as Rex's back was turned, Jess asked them what had happened.

'What are they saying, Jess?'

Jess turned to me, her face so white that it looked like it was made out of that plaster stuff you use to make models. I guess I knew what she was going to say before she opened her mouth, but I had this tiny hope in my heart that I was wrong.

She swallowed. Took a breath. 'Enclosure 17.'

I ran. Through the main room, out of the back door and down the winding path. All I could hear was the sound of my own heart thumping. I felt the gravel crunching under my feet and saw the blur of trees and bushes as I passed. But nothing mattered except getting to his enclosure.

I skidded to a stop at enclosure 17 and saw everything the same as it always was. The log I sat on the first time I saw him; the flattened patch of grass I always laid on when we hung out; his half-full water bowl with bits of leaf floating in it. And there was the place I always put his dinner bowl, and his little house.

But Mr Prickles wasn't waiting for me.

'Mr Prickles!' I called. 'It's me. I'm here.'

There was no movement from his house. No rustling in the straw.

'Alex.' I felt a hand on my shoulder. I hadn't even realised Jess was behind me.

I closed my eyes for a second, hoping that when I opened them I'd see his snuffly nose come quivering out of the doorway. But there was nothing.

'Mr Prickles!' I shouted, climbing over the fence into the enclosure. I knelt on the ground, putting my face to his doorway. I already knew, of course I did, but I had to try.

'Alex.' Jess climbed in after me. 'I'm so sorry.' Her huge blue eyes were full of tears. I thought I knew every one of Jess's looks: the classic eye roll; the single eyebrow raise; the double eyebrow raise; the glare; the frown; the I'm-about-to-kick-you stink eye; the trying-not-to-smile smile; and even the occasional full-burst-of-laughter smile. I had never seen her look at me like this. And it broke me.

I pulled my hat off my head and sobbed into it, so hard that I couldn't catch my breath. He was

Mr Prickles – the most adorable person in the world and my best buddy. He couldn't be gone. And he was.

I sank down on to the grass and cried while Jess hugged me. For some reason, I wasn't even embarrassed. I know super-agents are supposed to be brave and tough, and I obviously am massively both of those things, but I think you can be brave and tough and also sad. And I had never been so sad.

'I shouldn't have let this happen, Jess,' I said when the crying had eased off a bit. 'I should have protected him.'

'This is not your fault. Don't you dare blame yourself.'

'But he's so small, and gentle. I don't think he's ever done a mean thing in his life. This shouldn't have happened to him. It's not fair!'

'I guess life would be easier if bad things only happened to bad people.'

'If only Batman was here right now – he'd sort this out. He'd save Mr Prickles and bring the bad guys to justice.'

'Mr Prickles doesn't need Batman,' Jess said gently. 'He has you.'

I looked at Jess, her face all blurry through my tears, and I felt this surge of feeling towards her. In that moment, I truly realised how much she meant to me and how lucky I was to have her as a friend.

I squeezed her hand. 'No. He has us.'

There was no time to be miserable. We needed to be in butt-kicking mode and I knew exactly whose butt I was going to kick first. I found Rex by one of the far enclosures.

'Where is he, Rex? What happened to Mr ... the hedgehog from enclosure 17?'

'It died.'

I have never, ever wanted my ear to fart as badly as I did right then. It had to be a lie. It had to be.

The relief I felt when the rumble buzzed through my eardrum was so enormous that I nearly cried again. Rex was lying.

'Liar,' I said.

'I came down first thing this morning and found it dead. It must have gone into hibernation – I told you it was underweight.'

'Liar.' I shook my head. Why would he make up

something so awful? It was time to find out. 'Do you want to hear my theory, Rex?'

'Why would you have a theory?'

'Because the hedgehog from enclosure 17 isn't the only animal who has disappeared under mysterious circumstances, is he?'

'I don't know what you're talking about.' *Lie.*

'Six rabbits, nine hamsters, a fox, a tortoise, two cats and a hedgehog,' Jess said. 'In the past six months.'

'So what? You think I'm doing something to them?'

'Maybe not you, Rex, but I think you know who is,' I said.

'You're crazy. I don't know anything.' *Lie.*

'Why are you helping Taran?' I took a step closer to Rex and he backed up against a tree. 'We know he's taking the animals and someone here is helping him.'

'Taran's just the animal behaviourist. He doesn't even come out here.'

Me and Jess looked at each other. So that was why the animals didn't recognise The Rattler's scent or voice – Taran had never been out to the animal enclosures. We'd assumed he had, but thinking about it we'd only ever seen him at the front of the building or near the office. 'Maybe not during the day,' I said. 'But he comes at night, doesn't he?'

'Someone gives him the keys,' said Jess.

'And then there's you, with all your new expensive stuff,' I said. 'I don't think that's a coincidence.'

Rex looked from me to Jess and back again. 'Whatever you think Taran's done, it has nothing to do with me.' *Lie.*

'Then maybe we'd better check with your mum.'

For the first time since we'd confronted him, Rex looked really panicked. 'Don't talk to Mum.'

'Then tell us the truth,' Jess said.

'And tell us why,' I shouted. 'These animals have done nothing to you. You're supposed to care for them. Why would you betray them like that?'

'I didn't choose this life,' Rex shouted back. 'Mum chose it and I have to go along with everything she says.'

'So you secretly hate animals?' Jess said.

'I don't hate them. But I have to spend all my time looking after them. Mum doesn't make much money, so I have to go to school wearing rubbish clothes and getting picked on. It was bad at my last school but it's worse here with Jason Newbold and that lot, always giving me a hard time.'

'So when Taran offered to pay you if you helped him sneak in and take some animals, you thought you could get some cool gear and that would change everything?' I couldn't believe what I was hearing. A pair of trainers isn't going to make you fit in.

'I didn't think it was that bad. He's only taking them to his place so he can practise his training techniques on them,' Rex said.

Jess looked at me and I shook my head. Rex wasn't lying.

'That isn't what he's doing,' I said.

'He's doing cruel experiments on them. Hurting them,' said Jess.

'Killing them.' I took all of my strength not to think about what Taran might be doing to Mr Prickles. If I was going to rescue him, I needed to focus.

Rex looked shocked. 'I didn't know.'

'Well, you do now,' I said. 'So you're going to help us make it right.'

'I don't want anything to do with any of this,' said Rex.

'You were happy to be involved when you were getting paid,' Jess shouted, her cheeks bright pink. 'You vile piece of scum.'

Blimey.

'What have you two ever done for me?' Rex said. 'You helped me out once when Jason was having a go at me. Once. He calls me names every single day. I'm on my own at school every playtime, every lunchtime. And now you want my help? Well, you can't make me.'

'We'll tell your mum,' I said.

'I'll tell her you're lying and that I caught you throwing stones at the donkeys. She'll fire you.'

'Last chance, Rex,' I said. 'I'm warning you. You messed with my hedgehog and I have nothing left to lose.'

'What can you do?'

'Seen your phone, lately, Rex?' Jess said.

Rex looked horrified and dug his hand into his pocket, pulling out his iPhone. 'It's right here.'

A streak of grey launched itself out of the tree, smashing into Rex's shoulder and knocking the phone out of his hand. It clattered to the floor, making us all wince. It doesn't matter whose iPhone is dropped, it's never nice to see those majestic screens shattered. Rex bent down to grab it but another fuzzy grey shape flung itself at his arm, digging in with its sharp claws.

'Ow! Rex shouted. 'Get off me!' He shook his arm to try to loosen it, but the squirrel had an impressive grip. Another five or six squirrels leapt from the tree, bouncing off Rex and on to the ground, where they scattered and regrouped, going in for another attack and another.

While all this was happening, I grabbed Rex's phone. 'Thanks guys,' I said to the squirrels. One of them hopped on to Jess's shoulder and she gave it a peanut.

'What the hell is happening?' said Rex, as the squirrels finally released him and disappeared back into the tree. 'How did you do that?'

'You've upset a lot of people, Rex,' I said. 'And the animals are fighting back.'

'This is nuts.' He shook his head and rubbed his arm.

'Good one,' I said. 'Squirrels, nuts – and I thought I was the only puntertainer around here.'

'Give me my phone.'

'We'll give you your phone back once we've finished with it,' said Jess.

'You can't use it anyway, you don't know my password.'

'We don't need your password – we have another animal friend who's going to bite off your thumb so we can carry it around and use the print to unlock it whenever we want,' I said. Then I bent down and looked into the bushes. 'Here, Biter, Biter – we have a job for you.'

Rex turned pale and buried his hands into his armpits.

'Just kidding, Rex,' I laughed. 'You should have seen your face.'

'We know your password,' added Jess. 'We have spies everywhere, and you've been using your phone in front of a friend of ours.'

At that moment, Harry was probably busting some moves to his choice of show tunes and grime.

Rex looked around and swallowed.

I entered Rex's password and started scrolling through his messages. 'Oh look, texts from Taran arranging to meet up and exchange cash,' I said. 'And...'

I read the message again because I could hardly believe what I was seeing, but there it was in all of its slick-graphic horror, and we all know that technology never lies.

'You told him to go to enclosure 17. You told him to take Mr Prickles!'

I can hardly describe the rage I felt at that moment – like Hulk and Kylo Ren combined. I wanted to pick Rex up by his feet and smash him into the tree.

But Jess stepped in front of me. 'Remember the mission, Alex. Hurting Rex isn't going to get Mr Prickles back.'

'I thought he was just taking your hedgehog to another place like ours,' Rex said. 'I didn't know he was going to do anything bad to it.'

'My hedgehog,' I half smiled. Mr Prickles belonged with me and I was going to get him back. 'This is what we're going to do, Rex,' I said. 'We have your phone now. We can show these messages to your mum and she'll know what you've been up to, and I know you don't want that.'

'So we're holding on to it until we rescue the animals and stop Taran from taking any more,' said Jess. 'If you try to warn him, we'll tell on you.'

'And then your mum will probably send you to boarding school, or youth offenders, or to puppy bootcamp, or whatever.'

'Besides,' Jess said. 'I don't think you really wanted the animals to get hurt, and now that you know what's happening, I'm sure you want to do the right thing.'

Rex gave the smallest nod.

'As long as we're clear,' I said. 'You can go.'

Rex turned and crunched up the gravel path towards the house.

'Now,' Jess said. 'Let's go get your hedgehog back.'

# 21

## Smiling With the Enemy

We used Rex's phone to set up a meeting with Taran, a.k.a. The Rattler, a.k.a. the creep who I was going to end if I didn't get Mr Prickles back. The following day dragged by like Christmas Eve until we got to leave school and make our way to the sanctuary. We told Rex to get his mum out of the sanctuary by any means necessary and, as soon as they were gone, we got ready for our meeting with Taran. The trickiest part was that we needed animal assistance, but as soon as we told them it would involve being close to The Rattler, they were too frightened to volunteer. Finally, with the promise of sweet revenge on their nemesis, I managed to persuade a couple of them to help me out.

Five minutes before Taran was due to arrive, Jess took her position at the side of the building, hidden behind a bush, and I ran through my part in my head. I needed to keep Taran talking for as long as possible and I needed to get some information from him. I also had to act like I didn't have any beef with him, when actually I don't think I've ever hated anyone so much in my life.

At 4pm, the sanctuary doorbell rang. It was time.

I checked the rat in my pocket was OK, swallowing back a pang of sadness that it wasn't Mr Prickles in there. It was good in a way. It reminded me what was at stake. I opened the door.

'Oh, hi there, Alex,' Taran said. 'I was expecting Rex.'

'Hey, Taran.' I really hated his smug face. 'Rex is just doing something – he'll be back in a minute.'

'I'll just wait outside then.' Taran started to turn towards the garden where Jess was trying, in her usual elephant-like way, to sneak out of the gate.

'Wait!' I said. 'It looks like it's going to rain. You

should stay here – I'll hang out with you while you wait.'

'But…' Taran made a face.

'Unless you don't want to hang out with me for some reason?'

'Course I do, mate,' Taran smiled, and my ear farted loudly.

'Do you want to come out the back and see the animals?' I said.

'I don't go back there.'

'Why not?'

'It's to do with professional boundaries.' *Lie*. 'Is Jess here today?'

'Yeah, she's in crit care. There's a deer in there that got hit by a car or something.'

I watched his face.

'Oh, really?'

'Dreadful, isn't it?' I said. 'I mean, what kind of scumbag would do something like that?'

I saw something flash in his eyes, just for a second, but I couldn't tell if it was guilt about being an animal runner-overer, or anger with me for calling him a scumbag.

'Jess certainly seems to have a way with animals,' he said. Classic subject change.

'Yeah, she loves them, and she seems to understand them pretty well.' I tipped my head to one side in the most innocent way possible. 'Is that why you don't bring Meena here anymore?'

'What?' There was that look again.

'Because you think Jess is going to try to take her home, or something?' I did a smidle, which is what you call the sidling version of a smile.

'Yeah,' he fake laughed. Deep in my ear, a sound reverberated, and a stink seeped into the air. What was Taran's interest in Jess? And why would he lie about it?

'So maybe me and Jess could come to your place sometime, you know, to do some work experience with you.'

'But you're happy here, aren't you?' Taran sounded a tiny bit panicked.

'It's OK,' I said. 'But there are a lot of things that go wrong here. Like power cuts. Do you get those at your work?'

'We have a back-up generator,' Taran said. 'So when the power cuts out, it only takes a few seconds for the generator to kick in and we're back in business.'

'How convenient,' I said. 'And fancy. What do you do when an animal escapes?'

'They don't escape,' Taran said. 'We have secure doors. Unless the animals work out how to use a security card, they aren't going anywhere.'

'And that's to keep them safe, right?'

'Right.' *Lie.*

'Maybe I could recommend it to Rex's mum for this place,' I said. 'Can I see the card?'

'Sorry, Alex, I don't have it on me.'

My ear farted. I glanced over Taran from top to bottom. His skinny jeans were so tight that there was no way a security pass could be in one of those pockets, or if it was I would definitely be able to see it. That left his cardigan.

'No probs,' I said.

'I wonder what's taking Rex so long.' Taran took a step towards the front door. 'I might just wait outside, get some air.'

'Before you go,' I said. 'I've been meaning to ask you something.'

'What's that?' Taran looked worried. Which, to be fair, was understandable because I was acting like a bit of a maniac.

'Well, I want to dress a bit cooler, you know, to impress the ladies. And I've been thinking about getting a cardigan. I've seen one I like but it's

£29.99, which is all of my pocket money savings. Before I spend my cash, I wondered if I could try yours on?'

'Why don't you try one on in a shop?' Taran pulled his cardigan tighter around him.

'I'll let you in on a secret,' I said. 'I know I seem charmingly confident but I'm cripplingly shy, and when I get anxious, I get a bit of a stomach issue.'

'Eh?'

'You know, pain, wind, runny poo. It's very embarrassing.'

Taran's face just dropped. People never like talking about poo.

'And I get really intimidated in shops...' I let the stink do its work. 'So if I could just try yours on quickly, that would be awesome.'

Taran ripped his cardigan off and held it out to me, being careful not to make any physical contact.

'Thanks, Taran,' I said, pulling a sleeve over the arm of my overalls. 'You're the best!'

I said the last part clearly because it was a very important codeword.

At that moment, Harry the horse, who had been listening from around the corner, flew down the corridor towards us, ramming into Taran and knocking him off his feet. While he was distracted, a.k.a. cowering in fear in the corner of the room as Harry hoofed him in the chest with his tiny hooves, I felt around in the pockets of the cardigan. 'Look out, Taran, he's going for your face,' I shouted. As Taran shielded his face with his arms, I pulled the security card out and stuck it in my overalls. I nodded at Harry who gave Taran one last good kick and then moonwalked back through the sanctuary to the garden. It sounded like he was laughing.

'Tell Rex I'll text him,' said Taran, grabbing back his cardigan and legging it to the door.

'Will do, mate,' I said. 'Thanks for stopping by.'

A minute later, Jess ran back in.

I pulled the rat out of my pocket. 'Did you smell him?'

The rat squeaked.

'Can you confirm that it was The Rattler?'

Jess twitched. 'It was definitely the same person who's been taking the animals from the sanctuary.'

'Cheers Raymond, you were very brave.' I tickled Raymond on the back of his neck and walked through the sanctuary to put him back in his cage.

'Did you get it?' Jess asked.

'Mission accomplished,' I said, holding up the security pass. 'And you?'

'Meena was super helpful.' Jess held up the print out of the SPARC building layout that Dave had managed to get for us. There was now a red cross on one of the rooms. 'She hates being part of what Taran's doing but doesn't know how to stop him,' said Jess. 'She was more than happy to show me where the animals are kept. The trouble is it's a really complex building. We can't have a map in our pocket in case we're searched and I don't think either of us will be able to memorise the route.

'Ooh,' I said. 'I have a hack for that.'

# 22

## Showdown at the House of Horror

It was a dull November day. The sky was a mass of dark grey cloud and though it wasn't raining, it felt as though a storm was lurking just out of sight, waiting to pounce at any moment.

As we piled off the coach at the recycling plant, me and Jess hung back so we were last in line, with Dave just ahead of us.

'I wish it wasn't so gloomy,' said Jess. 'It feels like a sign that something bad's going to happen.'

'What are you talking about, Jessticles? This is perfect finale weather. Although it would be even better if the SPARC building was a tower with one of those metal spikes at the top so that it could get struck by lightning.'

'This isn't the movies, Alex. This is serious. What if we get caught?'

'We're just kids – what are they going to do to us?'

'Maybe the same things they do to the animals? Maybe spark us and make us brain dead?'

'It won't come to that,' I said, though I didn't entirely believe it. 'We've got each other, and we've got back up. We're taking that son of a biscuit down.'

'And we're getting Mr Prickles back.' Jess squeezed my hand – it was like she knew what I was thinking.

With Miss Fortress at the front and other teachers and parents at our side, we walked into the plant.

'So this is it, then,' said Jess.

'Yep. And we only get one shot.'

'Lucky you're so good under pressure, then.'

I smiled and put my arm around her, just as

Jason happened to look back. 'Alex Tramp-Hat and his freakish girlfriend are smooching in the back, Miss!'

'Jason, come to the front where I can keep an eye on you,' Miss Fortress snapped at him.

'Unfair,' he said, giving Miss Fortress a finger swear after she turned her back.

Dave looked at us over his shoulder and gave us a wink.

We stood in the entrance area of the recycling plant while a man with a clipboard wearing a neon yellow jacket bored on about how essential it is to treat confidential waste paper with respect. There were also some rules about how to behave in the potentially dangerous plant. Obviously I didn't listen to those.

Even though I'm an A-star agent, I'm not that great with directions and maps and stuff, so Dave was in charge of telling us where to go when we snuck off, and once we were inside the SPARC building, we had a trick up our sleeves, or rather taped to my belly in a sealed plastic bag. We were about halfway through the tour when Dave gave us the nod. Miss Fortress called the mum standing next to us up to the front to ask her something, and me and Jess slipped away through a side door into a warehouse area. It was a huge, grey, noisy space, filled with trollies and containers and forklift trucks. There were quite a few people around, but in such a big place and with so much going on, nobody noticed us walking in.

We ducked down behind some of those big plastic containers we saw on our reccy, took off our school jumpers and put on the high-vis waistcoats we had stuffed under our coats. Dave had made us some replica badges that looked so legit I reckon we could have used them to get into the White House. We clipped them to our coats.

'How are we going to get across the warehouse and out of the door without anyone stopping us?' Jess whispered.

'Easy,' I said. 'We wait until nobody's paying much attention and then we just go. If you do things with swag, people don't even think to question you. Hashtag life hack.'

We crouched behind the containers, watching. This was probably the easiest part of the mission, but if we didn't get it right, we'd fail before we'd even started. Jess looked super-nervous. My heart was racing.

'What are you doing?' Jess whispered. 'Are you trying not to puke?'

'Shush. I'm using the force.'

'Oh God, I really hope this isn't an important part of the plan. You know the force isn't real, right?'

'Just because you don't believe in it, doesn't mean it's not real,' I said.

'No, the fact that it's not real means it's not real.'

'If it's not real then how come it works?'

'If it worked then everyone would be using it all the time, Alex. Give me one example of it when it's worked.'

'I just used the force to make my heartbeat slower.'

Jess gave me one of her most fun-sucking looks. 'That's called calming down.'

'You can call it calming down if you're more comfortable with that.' I gave her a knowing smile.

'Why are you looking at me like that? You know the force is a made-up thing for a fictional world about imaginary people? You do actually know that?'

'Believe that if comfort you, it does,' I said in my best Yoda voice and patted her hand. 'And one more thing.' I peeped over the containers for one last check. 'It's time to move.'

We stood up and stepped out from behind the containers like it was the most normal thing in the world.

'Remember, Jessticles,' I said. 'We are the force and the force is with us.'

We walked across the warehouse towards the side exit. As we passed a stack of wheelie trolleys, I casually pulled at the handle of one. It made a bit of a clatter, like when you try to separate the trolleys at Sainsbury's, but nobody seemed to notice. Jess nodded at a pile of containers near the door and we moved towards them. I gave each one a push. None of them were empty but they would have to do.

'How do we get the box on the trolley?' I said. 'They look heavy.' I put my arms around one and heaved, but it had quite a lot of paper in it and weighed a tonne.

Jess sighed and pushed the trolley over to me.

'Don't try to lift it, Jess. It would take Superman riding an elephant to shift that thing.'

Jess slid the bottom of the trolley under the base of the container and tipped it towards her.

The container slid fully on to the trolley and Jess wheeled it to the exit door.

'The trolley must be magic,' I said, pushing the bar on the door and holding it open for her.

'No, I used the force.' Jess rolled her eyes at me. 'Come on.'

I wasn't sure how she'd managed to move it but I couldn't allow myself to be beaten by Jess. I gave the nearest container a shove, just to test my strength. Unfortunately, that one wasn't as heavy as the one on our trolley and it started to tip towards the container next to it.

'She's gonna blow!' I said, pushing Jess the rest of the way out of the door just as the container fell onto the next one, which fell onto the next, and the next, and the next, like in those domino things people set up to film for funny home-movie shows. It made a right noise.

'Alex!' Jess hissed at me as the door swung shut behind us.

'No time to discuss this now,' I said. 'We have an important mission to complete. Let's put it to the back of our minds and never mention it again.' I marched forward towards the SPARC building. Jess huffed and followed.

We walked together up the ramp to the darkened glass door of SPARC. It rose up in front of us in a pretty sinister way – there's something so creepy about knowing people can see you when you can't see them. But with that in mind, I didn't hesitate. I pushed open the door like there was no reason in the world why I shouldn't be entering a top-secret facility disguised as a confidential-waste recycler.

'Morning, mate,' I said to the security guard at the front desk. Well, I say desk but it was more of a bullet-proof booth, surrounded by glass and with a speaker so we could talk to each other. Either side of the booth was a glass wall, separating the entrance area from the rest of the building. There was no way of getting through except a door in the glass that had some fancy security gadget flashing on it. The only way through was to be buzzed in by the guard.

The guard looked us over. 'You from next door?' he said.

'Yep. Here to collect your confidential paper waste,' I nodded with the confidence of Quicksilver – the one from the X-men franchise, not the Avengers' franchise, because he's dead, obvs.

'Aren't you a bit young to be working at the plant?' he frowned at us.

'We're on work experience,' I said.

'Aren't you a bit young to be on work experience?'

'You're not the first person to have said that to us.' I looked over at Jess with my eyebrows raised. 'Right?'

Jess nodded in a very guilty way.

'My friend here looks very young for her age, you see. On account of her being so extremely tiny, and her eyes being the size of a bush baby's and her hair looking like a toddler tried to style it.'

'And you?' The guard looked me up and down.

'I'm like one of those child geniuses you hear about – I was moved up in school a few years. I'm like a young Professor Brian Cox or Stephen Hawking.'

'Then why are you doing work experience in a recycling plant?'

I actually hadn't expected that question. 'Um, I have a thing for paper.'

The guard frowned.

'Look, we have ID if you want to check.' Jess dangled her pass in front of the glass. The guard was sitting on a high chair, so he was raised up above us.

'Empty your pockets,' the guard said and he watched as we turned them inside out, spilling sweet wrappers and bits of tissue onto the shiny tile floor.

'I'll have to search you,' he tutted and got down off his stool. 'Wait there.'

We'd expected this, and the next part of the plan was key. We couldn't let him discover what I had strapped to my body. He pressed a button in his booth, which opened the door, then he walked out to look at our passes properly and pat us down. He'd only got one step into the room when he sniffed and made a horrified face. All my lies had whizzed up an especially disgusting stink.

'Oh, no. I think it's happening again!' I said, clutching at my stomach.

'Where's the bathroom?' Jess asked the guard. 'He's not feeling well.'

The guard looked at me like he wanted to push me out of the door with a stick.

'I don't know if I can hold it.' I jiggled up and down and looked at the guard. 'I need the toilet right now!'

'You stay here,' the guard said to Jess as he held the door open for me. 'I'll take you to the gents but you'll have to stay under my supervision at all times.'

'Even in the cubicle?' I said as I scuttled through.

'No, not in the cubicle, I'll wait outside.' The guard made sure the door closed behind us and then led me around the corner.

I made sure to be as noisy as possible and take plenty of time pretending to do my business so that Jess could carry out the next part of the plan. As soon as me and the guard – who we should really give a name, let's call him Kevin – as soon as me and Kevin disappeared from sight, she would have given the signal to our back up. That meant that the power should be going down any time… A click and a shudder was followed by sudden quiet and darkness.

'What happened?' I shouted from the cubicle.

'It's a power cut,' said Kevin. 'I should just go and check…'

'Don't leave me!' I said in my most scaredy voice.

'Don't worry, it's been happening a lot lately.

The back-up generator should start up in a few seconds.'

I counted to three, hoping that Jess would have enough time to execute stage five, and then the lights clicked back on. I flushed the toilet.

'Are you done now? I need to take you back to reception and check your badges before I can let you in for the collection,' Kevin said.

'Just a sec,' I said. 'This needs a double flush.'

I stepped out of the cubicle and walked over to the sinks to wash my hands, when suddenly the most awful noise sounded out in the corridor.

'Er, is that the back-up generator?' I said.

'No.' Kevin darted towards the door. 'It sounds like animals. I need to get you back to reception so I can investigate.'

'I need to go again!' I said, rushing back into the cubicle. 'I might need a little while.'

The noises outside were getting louder. Of course *I* knew that Jess used the few moments when the power was out and the cameras down to let herself and half of The Storm's army into the building and through the security door. There were dogs, foxes, rats, cats, rabbits, snakes and frogs creating havoc through SPARC central.

'Are there animals running wild in the building?' I said through the toilet door.

'Just stay put and I'll be back once I've figured out what's going on.' I heard Kevin's footsteps as he ran across the bathroom and the slam of the door as it closed behind him. I unbuttoned the bottom of my shirt, tiptoed to the door and peered into the corridor. All clear. Right on time, Jess came squeaking around the corner towards me.

'You OK in there, Bob?' Jess said, waving at him.

He was swimming in a large, clear plastic bag, which we'd sealed with just a straw poking out to provide a bit of air and taped to my tummy. There wasn't much space but it was the only way we could get him in unseen. To stop him getting bored we'd put in some gravel samples that he wanted to examine so he could choose one for his new tank. They jiggled about in the bottom of the bag. With his photographic memory, Bob was the only person who could guide us through the building to the lab.

'I thought we'd better keep the trolley and container in case anyone else sees us,' Jess said.

'Hopefully they won't bother to check with security.'

'Good thinking, Teenado.'

'Teenado? Really?'

'Like a teeny tornado. Teenado.'

'Yeah, makes total sense now,' said Jess. 'According to Bob, there should be a door on the left at the end of this corridor. We need to go through it to get to the lifts.'

As we walked towards the lifts, I peered into some of the rooms that had been abandoned when the animals stormed the building.

'Woah, look at the mess The Storm's army has left!'

There were dropped coffee cups, stacks of paper all over the floor, overturned chairs and general chaos.

Jess pointed at a chewed-up shoe. 'At least Biter's having fun.'

'So, hopefully, they've led everyone to the other side of the building by now.'

'Yes, our path should be clear for a few minutes.'

We pressed the button on the lift and waited. It seemed to take forever for the doors to slide open, and even longer for them to close again. Jess pressed the button to take us down to the basement.

'Are you sure Meena was telling the truth about the lab being underneath the building?' I asked.

'Not one hundred per cent,' said Jess. 'But I trust her.'

'I can't even remember what that's like,' I said. 'Just to take someone's word for something, to believe them without proof.'

'That's kind of sad.'

'Yeah, I guess.'

'I miss being able to connect with animals without using my power,' Jess said. 'To have a bond with them even though I can't know exactly what they're saying. You know, like you have with Mr Prickles.'

'Life was definitely simpler before we met The Professor.'

We stood in silence for a moment as the lift kept moving down, deeper and deeper beneath the ground.

'Would you want to go back to the way things were?' Jess said.

'Nah. You?'

'No. It would mean losing too much.' She turned to me and smiled, just as the lift pinged to a stop.

'Game faces on,' I said, as the doors parted to reveal what was waiting for us on the other side.

# 23

## We Meet at Last

We heard him before we saw him, his voice sharp.

'No, the operation has been compromised. The whole area is swarming with reporters and I cannot afford to be seen. I need immediate extraction.'

In front of us stood a man, tapping his foot and hammering at the lift button. I was about to tell him what Mum always tells me – that pressing the button a gazillion times doesn't make the lift come any quicker – but something stopped me.

The man looked about my dad's age. He had curly hair – dark but with some grey in it – and a short grey beard. He was wearing a suit and tie, and shiny black shoes – so smart that he looked like he should be in one of those swanky flats at the top of a skyscraper, with a balcony looking over the lights of the city. Behind and slightly to each side of him stood a huge, completely bald man and a woman with her hair pulled back so tightly that it looked like her face might split up the middle. Big baldy looked like a thug, and stretch-face looked mean – like an assassin. And the guy in the middle looked … familiar.

I heard Jess let out a tiny gasp as she recognised him. At the same time, baldy and stretchy noticed us in the lift and stepped closer to the middle guy, their hands shooting to their belts. Middle guy's eyes widened as he took us in. His eyes were dark and bright, and I swear they flashed silver for the quickest moment. It's hard to explain exactly what it was about them that was so disturbing, but it was like once he'd seen you he'd never forget you. The last time I saw those eyes was on a photo in Miss Smilie's office.

It was Montgomery McMonaghan.

'Identify yourselves,' assassin lady said.

'Recycling collectors from the plant next door,' I said, with a cheery smile, while trying to focus on controlling my ear farts and hoping that Bob was fully covered by my shirt. We really didn't need to draw any extra attention to ourselves.

All three of them frowned.

'We're on work experience.' I pointed to my badge. 'Security cleared us.'

Assassin lady pulled a phone from her inside jacket pocket. 'I'm going to get confirmation. Names?' She looked hard at me and Jess. I tried to look totally chill but I was worried that if Montgomery McMonaghan heard our names, he would remember them from all the PALS stuff. Miss Smilie must have told him about us.

'I'm Alan,' I said, playing for time. 'And this is J...' I tried to think of a different girl's name beginning with J, but instead I came up with '... Jeremy'.

One corner of Montgomery McMonaghan's mouth twitched up in a half smile. 'Your name is Jeremy?'

'Her parents really wanted a boy,' I said. My ear was desperate to fart and the strain of keeping it under control was making me sweat. 'She was quite a disappointment to them.'

Assassin Tight-Face started scrolling through her phone for a number. If she checked our story, there was no way we'd not get caught. I tried to think. I could almost feel Jess panicking beside me. It was like invisible smoke coming off her, forming the word 'help!' above her head.

Montgomery McMonaghan's eyes flicked from me to Jess and back again, that side of his mouth curling upwards in amusement. It was like he *knew*.

Tight-Face clicked on a number and put the phone to her ear. It was so quiet that I could hear the phone ringing at the other end. Our only hope was to run but the thought of leaving that building without Mr P made me feel sick. I weighed up my options. What would super-spy Nick Fury do? Better to escape and make a new plan than to get caught and be imprisoned and tortured or killed. Abort.

I lifted my hands, my right to shove the trolley at McMonaghan and my left to punch the 'doors closed' button.

'Forget it, Evangeline,' Montgomery McMonaghan

said, without taking his eyes off me and Jess. 'We don't have time for this. We have the long game to think about. Let's go.'

Tight-Face ended the call and the three of them moved to the side of the corridor so me and Jess could get our trolley out of the lift. We needed to get out of there as quickly and casually as possible. Unfortunately, one of the trolley wheels got caught in the crack between the lift and the floor, and Jess had to try to wiggle it free while I made sure the container didn't fall off. Not our finest agent moment. At last it was free and we squeaked out of the lift and down the corridor while McMonaghan and his bodyguards stepped into the lift.

'Nice hat, Alan,' he said, and I turned around to see him smiling at us – all perfect white teeth and flashing eyes. It was the smile of a madman. The lift doors closed and our arch enemy zoomed upwards.

'I'm texting Miss Fortress to tell her to stay out of sight,' Jess said, tapping away at her phone. 'That was probably the most frightening moment of my entire life.'

'Weally?' I said. 'Wann't cared a awl.'

'Why are you talking weird?'

The truth was that my mouth was drier than a camel's knee because terror had sweated all the moisture out of my body. I swallowed a couple of times and smacked my lips a bit.

'Just practising my accents for our next undercover mission,' I said.

Jess sniffed and raised an eyebrow.

'We'll talk about this later once we've got the animals out. Let's get on with the plan, shall we? We must be nearly there now.'

We turned right halfway down the corridor and reached a double door made of blackened glass, with a security scanner next to it.

'Here goes.' I took Taran's card out of my pocket and held it up to the light. There was a beep, and the light turned green. We pushed the door open.

'Woah,' Jess said, looking around at the room, which was quite clearly an evil laboratory.

It was large – like the size of our school dining hall – and shaped like a wrong-way-round 'L', with the vertical part stretching in front of us and then a sharp right corner with another section beyond. Everything was made of metal. There were shiny countertops, covered with equipment: trays of instruments including small blades; metal rods and wires with suction pads attached; football-sized metal spheres, with sparks jumping off them; machines with vertical belts that whizzed round in a circle creating static electricity.

The only sound was a kind of low buzzing, crackling electrical noise – like a malfunctioning lightsaber.

'There's no way anything good is happening here,' Jess said, and as I turned to reply, strands of Jess's hair started to float upwards, like what happens when you rub your head with a balloon.

'Let's keep moving,' I said. 'We need to find the animals.'

In the centre of the room was a large steel table, and as we walked towards it, I could see that it was spattered with drops of blood and clumps of animal fur. It made me feel sick.

'I can hear something,' Jess whispered, staring at the torture table in horror. 'It's quiet. I think it's the animals … this way.' She pulled me where the room turned right. This section of the room was different. It had fridges full of tiny bottles and jars, and a messy desk covered with food wrappers and papers, and a couple of different computers. Above it was a whiteboard full of equations and symbols. I had no idea what any of it meant. In the furthest wall to the right was another door with a security pad. I held up the card and the door swished to the side, letting us see into the room behind it.

'Oh my God,' Jess said.

The room was full of cages. There were hundreds of them, lining every wall and stacked from floor to ceiling. The larger ones had metal bars, and others – the ones which held the smaller animals – were made of glass. And almost every cage held an animal. None of them were making any noise. It was freezing cold in the room and there wasn't any bedding in the cages, so most of the animals were huddled in their corners, shaking or rocking. Some were completely still. Many of them were painfully skinny and had visible wounds. It was so awful that if I'd let myself stand there a moment longer, I would have cried.

'Alex,' Jess said, her lips trembling and tears trickling down her face. 'What do we do? How can we help them all?'

I took a deep breath. 'We pull ourselves together,' I said. 'And do the job we came here to do.'

I stepped into the room and cleared my throat. 'Hi, everyone,' I said in a loud voice. 'My name is Alex. This is Jess. We're here to help you.'

There was movement in the cages, as lots of furry and scaly heads turned to look at us.

'We're going to open your cages,' said Jess. 'Those of you who are able to walk or run without help, jump out and head for the fire escape on the ground floor – down this corridor, left, right and left again. We've propped open the doors between here and there, and the fire escape will open if you push the bar. You'll find a flight of stairs upwards, then another door and then you'll be out.'

'If you prefer, you can disappear once you've escaped and go wherever you like – out into the wild or back to your family,' I said. 'But if you want our help, we can take you to a safe place.'

'Run around the back of this building to the one next door. You'll see a coach parked in the side-road and there will be a tall, dark-haired boy standing at the back of it. He'll hide you in the boot so we can get you away.'

'I know you're scared and in pain,' I said. 'But try to be quick and quiet.'

Jess twitched and turned to me. 'Some of them

are worried it's a trick. They don't know if they can trust us.'

'I can clear that up,' I said. 'Does anyone know where Mr Prickles is? He's a hedgehog, about this…' (I gestured with my hands) '…long. He's brown, spiky and completely adorable.'

Jess jolted a bit and pointed. 'Over there.'

As we ran over, I allowed myself a tiny moment of hope. Mr Prickles was alive. I scanned the cages but I couldn't see him. And then I heard a snuffle and a tiny, soft squeak. A black nose quivered out of the shadows in the corner of the cage. And the happiness I'd felt a second before shattered as I saw what they'd done to him.

He was shaking. He could hardly lift his head, and he looked so much smaller. At first I couldn't work out why, but when I looked closer I saw. It was so bad that I said the worst swear I could think of, then bit my lip to stop myself from crying. It didn't work.

Mr Prickles didn't have prickles anymore. His back was just brown skin, all wrinkled and exposed, like a snail without his shell. The fur on the rest of his body was thin and patchy and there were raised red lumps that looked sore as hell. I've never seen anything so horrific in my whole life.

'Alex.' Jess squeezed my hand. She was crying too. 'I know this is hard but we have to focus right now. We have to get them out.'

I opened the cage and reached my hand towards him. 'Mr Prickles,' I whispered. 'I've come to take you home.'

He started to drag his little body towards me so I gently scooped him up, trying to avoid touching his wounds and held him close to my face so he could see me.

'I'm so sorry. I'm so sorry I let this happen to you.' A tear rolled down my nose and he licked it off with his little tongue then nuzzled me with his snout.

'He says it's not your fault,' Jess said. 'And that he's missed you so much.'

I pulled my hat off my head and put him inside it.

It was obviously enough to convince the other animals that we were friends, because they started pulling themselves up and coming to the doors of their cages.

I nodded at Jess. 'Let's get these cages open.'

We ran from cage to cage, opening doors. There was no way I was putting Mr Prickles down anywhere, so I worked one-handed while carrying him inside my hat tucked in my left arm. In one of the first cages I opened, I found Piper. She had some kind of goo oozing out of her ear, but other than that she looked OK. She hopped around the floor, nudging on the other animals and leading them towards the exit. Many of the animals felt able to make their own way out, even those who looked so hurt that I was surprised they could even move. But some of them couldn't. And there was a tortoise who must have been Sir Blimmo. He was doing his best, but realistically wasn't going to make it up the stairs.

'Let's get them into the container and load it on to the trolley,' Jess said.

The container we'd brought with us didn't have much room inside it but I spied another one near the only desk in the room. When I lifted the lid, I could see there was only a small pile of paper at the bottom.

'Jess,' I called. 'We'll use this one – it's almost empty.'

As I passed it to Jess, I noticed photos stuck up

all around the desk of Taran posing for selfies with celebrities from reality TV.

'Ugh.' Jess rolled her eyes as she ran over with the trolley, avoiding the rabbits, lizards and other animals who were running for the door, and together we swapped the containers over. Then we pushed the container into the animal room and tipped the trolley so that it was almost horizontal.

'I'm sorry, guys, this isn't going to be very comfy,' I said. 'But it's the best we can do.'

Then Jess and I went from cage to cage, starting with the biggest and moving down to the smallest, lifting the animals out and carrying them to the container. The largest animal was a beagle whose paws were so swollen that he couldn't put weight on any of them.

'This might hurt a little,' said Jess. 'But once we're out of here, we'll get you fixed up. If you can just be brave and hold on for a bit longer.'

When all of the animals had either made their own way out or were safely in the recycling container, we closed the lid and wheeled it out of the room of caged horror and back into the main room of torment at the same time that someone ran in through the other door, slamming it behind him.

He spun around and stopped dead when he saw us. 'Alex. Jess. What are you doing here?'

'Taran!' I said. 'You son of a biscuit!' (FYI, I didn't say biscuit, I said another, much ruder word). I was so angry that I forgot to be scared.

Jess put the trolley down and flew at him, punching him with her tiny fists, and when that didn't hurt him as much as she wanted, she started kicking him in the shins with her boots. Under normal circumstances I would have joined in, but I was holding Mr Prickles and she totally had it under control anyway.

'Jess!' Taran shouted. 'Get off! I'm injured!' He shoved her away and I saw that he had blood pouring down his arm and dripping onto the floor.

'Woah, Jess – you bad-A!' I said.

'That wasn't me.' Jess was breathing heavily and so mad she was shaking. 'Though I wish it was.'

'It was a mangy fox,' Taran snapped. 'I was in the canteen getting a breakfast wrap and it attacked me. Get out of my way, I need some bandages and a tetanus jab.'

As you probably know, I hate blood, but seeing Taran in so much pain didn't upset me as much as it should have.

'You deserved to be bitten, you maniac,' I shouted. 'How could you do that to the animals? They've done nothing to you.'

'And they can't fight back. They can't report you,' Jess said. 'It's despicable to do this to them, you … you…'

'You're just boring me now,' Taran said, pushing past us and rummaging in a cupboard. 'I take it you're the ones responsible for letting in the animals that are rampaging through the building.'

'They hate you,' I said. 'They would have found a way in eventually. We just helped them along a bit.'

'So tell me how it is that you can understand how they feel and what they think?' He held a wad of cotton wool against the bite on his arm. 'I'm thinking that there's more to you and Jess than meets the eye.'

'You don't know anything about us,' Jess said.

'Oh, I know plenty,' Taran smirked. 'I know you can communicate with animals, Jess. And Alex, I'm not sure exactly what you can do, but I reckon you've got some kind of secret power, too.'

I didn't know what to say. Nobody had ever come close to guessing about us before. How could he know? Was he bluffing?

'And I don't think you came across these powers by yourselves, either. I think someone is helping you.'

'We don't need anyone's help,' Jess said. 'We manage perfectly well on our own. You're talking rubbish. Just like all that stuff you said about loving animals and wanting to help them.'

'Helping animals doesn't buy you a house, though, or a nice car,' Taran shrugged. 'My boss pays me very well for my work.'

'You do this just for the money?' Jess shrieked.

'Like I said, I get paid *a lot*.'

'By Montgomery McMonaghan,' I said. 'He pays you to try out his crazy science ideas on the animals.'

'That's the thing, Alex. His ideas aren't crazy – they work. They just need to be extensively tested on living subjects.' He finished tying a bandage over the cotton wool on his wound and then rested his fingertips on the metal counter. 'And he'll be really pleased to know I've caught him two new bodies to experiment on.'

He picked up two metal rods that had been attached to one of the electrical gadgets.

'These have rubber handles, so I can hold them without getting shocked,' he said. 'But the other ends, well, let's just say that when they touch you it's going to hurt like hell.'

He paced towards us with the rods, which were crackling and sparking.

'You see, my boss knows quite a lot about you two. He's been watching you for weeks.'

'How has he been watching us?' I said, trying to keep Taran talking so I could think of a plan. I could feel a strange rubbing sensation against my belly. I wasn't sure what Bob was doing, but I hoped it was something day-saving, because we were in *serious* trouble.

'Electrically enhanced spies,' Taran said. 'They're here somewhere, actually.' He glanced around the room. 'Come out guys.'

'Electrically enhanced?' Jess looked confused.

'Yes! Robots! Cool!' I looked around the room for them. Then I heard the clicking of claws on the hard floor and I looked down to see...

'Boris and Noodle!' Jess seemed as surprised as I was.

'What the heck?' I said.

'These two aren't ordinary guinea pigs,' Taran said. 'They've had some treatment, and as a result they're incredibly intelligent. Mr McMonaghan planted them in your school after the PALS disaster, and they've been watching you ever since. They were also tasked with stopping that pesky runaway cat who's been causing us so much trouble.'

'But how do they tell you what they've seen?' Jess asked.

'I developed a machine. A computer that uses symbols and pictures to represent words. The guinea pigs press the symbols and I know exactly what they're saying.'

'So they type with their little paws?' I started to laugh. There is nothing funnier than seeing an animal paw do a human job. But Boris and Noodle, though! I couldn't get my head around it. 'I had no idea, did you, Jess?'

'None,' she shook her head.

'You know what this means?' I said. 'That a couple of guinea pigs are better spies than us. I'm so ashamed right now.'

'You're still a jerk, Boris,' Jess glared at him.

'Anyway, the boss will be very pleased to hear I

have you caged. Then he can find out exactly what is going on in those brains of yours.' He tapped the sticks together and sparks flew off them.

We backed towards the cage room. It was a dead end, but we couldn't get past him to the door without risking extreme electrocution. The rubbing on my belly had got faster and stronger. I heard a tiny pop and a gush of fluid started trickling down my trousers and onto the floor.

'Have you wet yourself?' Taran said, looking horrified. 'You are without a doubt the most disgusting thing I have ever come across. And I work with rats and pond slime.' He laughed at his own joke.

Me and Jess looked at each other. I wasn't sure what Bob's plan was, but Taran was getting close we were going to have to run at him, both of us at the same time. That way at least one of us might get away.

'If I don't make it, look after Mr Prickles for me,' I said to her, preparing to charge.

Just as we launched ourselves towards Taran and his electrical rods of death, I heard a loud bark and a brown and black blur bounded into the room, leaping at Taran from behind. Taken by surprise, he slipped in the puddle of water that had been pooling on the floor and fell forwards, putting his hands out to break his fall. The rods slid in his grasp so that his hands were touching the metal. That made him scream. But when the ends hit the water, he let out the most disturbing sound I had ever heard. Way, way worse than the foxes. He crashed into a stack of cages and they tumbled down on top of him.

'Damn Bob, you are one smart fish,' I said, watching Taran flailing around under the cages.

'Quick!' Jess said. 'Alex! Meena! Come on!'

We ran out of the cage room and shut the door behind us, just as Taran started to emerge from the cages.

'The desk,' I gasped. We ran over to Taran's desk and pulled it in front of the door, just in time. Taran was up now and pushing at the door to get out.

'Meena!' he shouted. 'Bad dog. Protect your master!'

But Meena just growled at him.

'The door won't hold for long,' Jess said. 'We need to get out of here now.' She ran to the trolley and lifted it. 'Grab Boris and Noodle.'

'They've gone,' I said. 'And Bob's running out of water.'

'Then let's go.'

'One sec,' I said. We might not have time to search for the evidence to get the lab closed down, but there was one thing I could do to ruin Taran's plans. I emptied out his desk drawers, like a policeman on a raid looking for illegal substances. It was quite fun, actually. Then I spotted what I was looking for in the corner of a tray: a huge bunch of keys. I shoved them in my pocket then grabbed the other trolley handle. As quickly and carefully as we could, Jess and I wheeled it out of the room and back to the lift, with Meena behind us, guarding the rear. Nobody appeared while we waited for the lift, and as we stepped in and watched the doors close behind us, I looked down at Bob. He'd used a piece of gravel to pierce a hole in his bag and now he was struggling in a few centimetres of water.

'Bob's running out of time,' I said. 'And we didn't collect any evidence against Taran.'

'But we got the animals out, and that was the most important thing. Saving lives has got to come before everything else.'

I peeped on Mr Prickles who was sleeping in my hat. 'You're right, Jess, but I wish we could do something to stop Taran from doing this ever again.'

'Let's get out of here and back to the coach. We'll take the back fire exit to make sure all the animals got out alright, find some water for Bob, and then we can think. Maybe Bob will come up with something.'

The lift dinged and the doors slid open. The corridors were full of people drinking coffee and gossiping, or picking up fallen filing cabinets and wiping up spillages. A couple of them glanced at us but didn't look twice. We walked through them like we were supposed to be there, and then left through the back door. Somehow we'd pulled off the impossible mission.

# 24

## Code Red

As the fire exit swung shut behind us I took a breath, enjoying the feel of the freezing, wet wind stinging my face. We whipped off our neon waistcoats and stuffed them under our coats, then we pushed the trolley around the back of SPARC and the recycling plant until we could see the coach. The storage part was open and the driver was nowhere to be seen.

'Looks like Dave got them all in,' Jess said, just as Dave spotted us and gave us a wave. 'Just this last few to go, then we're done.'

'The worst thing about this trolley,' I said, as we stepped out into the open and towards the coach, 'is that it's impossible for me to do a cool gangster walk while I'm pushing it.'

'I would say that's the best thing about this trolley.'

Suddenly, Dave started gesturing at us in a mad kind of way, and pointing towards the front of the coach. We turned to see Miss Fortress leading the rest of Year 6 out of the plant and towards the side street, and the driver coming from the opposite direction. We were exposed – there was no way we'd be able to get the animals into the coach without being seen.

Then we heard a bark. Not Meena's deep woof, but a yappy, high-pitched sound, and a familiar animal trotted down the road.

'What the hell is my dog doing here?' Jason shouted. 'Quick, catch her!'

The chaos that followed as a bunch of kids, teachers, parents and a coach driver ran around trying to catch Fleur was the distraction we needed to get the trolley into the coach. Once the animals were loaded, I looked down to see an empty plastic bag and Bob flapping about, unable to breathe. There was no time to think. I looked around and saw a giant puddle in the road where the badgers had been up to their sabotaging ways. I placed Mr Prickles on the ground, ran for it and leapt in, releasing Bob from the bag. When I play it back in my mind, I like to see it in slow-mo, with explosions going off in the background and my muscles busting through my shirt.

Miss Fortress was hurrying the class onto the coach but Jess ran over. She scooped Bob into a travel coffee cup and helped me out of the hole.

The drive back to Cherry Tree Lane seemed to take forever, especially because the mum helpers made me take my wet trousers off and sit on the coach with one of their cardies wrapped around my legs like a skirt. It was home time when we finally turned into Cherry Tree Lane. Miss Fortress arranged for Jess and me to be dropped off at the sanctuary, and she kept the driver chatting while we unloaded the animals and snuck them through the green gate. Once the gate was closed, we ran inside.

'Code Red,' I shouted. 'We have a Code Red situation. Multiple casualties!'

Rex and his mum came running to the door,

their mouths falling open in shock when they saw me, Jess and the animals.

'Where did these animals come from?' Mrs Fernandes said. 'And what happened to your trousers?'

'We rescued them from a lab.' Jess opened the lid of the container to show her the animals inside. 'Some of them are in a really bad way.'

'Right.' Mrs Fernandes rolled up her sleeves. 'We'll need a vet. Jess, run to the office. Next to the phone on the desk you'll see a list of contact numbers. Call through the vets on the list and see if any of them are able to come out urgently.'

Jess nodded and ran off.

'Alex, wheel this trolley through to critical care and then fetch warm water, clean towels and fresh bedding. Then cover yourself up for goodness sake.'

I picked up the trolley and started pushing.

'Rex,' she said. 'Pheeeeee-wooooooow.' It was the most ear-splitting whistle I've ever heard.

Rex came and helped me with the trolley and we ran through the sanctuary to the critical-care shed.

I was still mad with Rex, so I didn't say a word

to him until I heard him sniff. I looked across to see that he was crying.

'Are you OK?' I said.

'I'm so sorry. I didn't know he was doing this to the animals. If I'd known, I never would have helped him.'

He wasn't lying.

'I know,' I said. 'Let's just concentrate on getting them better.'

The next couple of hours were frantic. Between the four of us, we got all the animals into enclosures, fed and comfortable. The more seriously wounded were examined by a vet who left medication and instructions for looking after them. Though a couple of them were in a really bad state, we were hopeful that with the right care they'd make a full recovery.

Me and Jess stayed late, and by the time we were stood at the front door waiting for my mum to collect us, we were proper done in.

'You two did well today,' Mrs Fernandes said, giving us a nod and then disappearing out the back.

'I suppose that's the closest we're ever going to come to her liking us,' Jess said.

'I'll take it,' I smiled. 'Let's go home. I'm starving.'

'Wait.' Rex came running into the room. 'I found these in the bottom of the box that was carrying the animals. I thought they might help.'

He held out a stack of papers covered in wee and poo stains, and also print and photographs. I could see pictures of animals, clearly in pain, with details of the experiments being carried out on them written underneath. There were also lists: names and addresses of the rescue centres and sanctuaries that Taran had used to get hold of his victims and a print out of the names and addresses of the pets he'd stolen who were microchipped.

'This. Is. Awesome,' I said.

'We can shut him down for sure!' Jess flicked through the sheets. 'We just need to get this in front of the right people.'

Rex nodded and turned to leave.

'You know, Rex,' I said. 'You should talk to your mum and explain how sad you've been. Sure, she's a bit weird and obsessed with animals, but my mum's obsessed with David Beckham – I swear she looks at her calendar of him more than she looks at my baby pics – and it doesn't mean she doesn't love me. I think your mum will listen and that she'll want to help.'

'Thanks,' Rex said. 'See you at school.' And he disappeared back down the corridor.

'So how are we going to get these papers to people who can actually do something about them?' I said. 'We know we're being watched now, and we can't risk Miss Fortress being identified.'

'We can't go to the police, either, because we know Montgomery McMonaghan has friends in high places.'

'We need to get the evidence to somebody who can fight the fight for us without us being involved.'

'It's not like you not to want the credit, Alex,' Jess raised an eyebrow.

'I know,' I said. 'And I deserve the credit, of course. But this is too important and too dangerous to mess up.'

'I have an idea,' said Jess. 'Let's send a message to The Storm.'

# 25

## Aftermath

'He did it, then,' I said, as the local news report ended. 'He delivered the evidence to the right people. And he brought Dexter back to us.'

Dexter had been delivered to the sanctuary, badly hurt, but alive. He was still in recovery there, getting stronger each day. The only lasting damage was that he'd lost a toe on the other foot. He didn't mind though – he said it was like a badge of honour for defending his family. By which I think he meant Miss Fortress. The Storm had come through.

'I knew he would.' Jess sipped on her soy hot chocolate like it was the nicest drink ever, which we all knew it wasn't because it was made of soy. 'The Storm is a cat of his word.'

'Have you seen him since he took the papers?'

'No. He's gone into hiding. Probably planning his next battle.'

'At least he's stopped trashing the town. I kind of miss his mardy face,' I said. 'Even though he's turned into a freedom-fighting, genius leader of the animal world and got a sick new name, he'll always be Colin to me.'

'I think we'll see him again. Taran might have been arrested and charged, but The Storm will want to make sure that Taran never hurts another animal. He'll be waiting to see what happens to him.'

'They're saying the maximum sentence is four years. Totally not long enough.' I licked the cream off the top of my normo hot chocolate. 'Not for what he's done.'

'And Montgomery McMonaghan got away again.'

'I've been thinking about that,' I said. 'And the fact that he was there, removing all the evidence at just the right time. He knew we were coming.'

'Yeah. He's always one step ahead of us,' Jess sighed.

'He arranged to have a bunch of kids lobotomised and ordered someone to torture hundreds of animals. But nobody knows except us.'

'If he'd been arrested for animal cruelty, he wouldn't have been properly punished anyway. Look at Taran – if he hurt people the way he hurt those animals, he'd be in prison for the rest of his life,' said Jess. 'It seems that different lives have different values in this world, and an animal's life isn't worth much at all.'

'But we did what we could,' I said. 'We saved all those lives. And that's something.'

'Yeah, it is,' Jess smiled. Then she started to twitch.

'What is it now?' I said.

'It's the water temperature,' said Jess. 'In the new, bigger tank, and with the furniture and Elle being there, it's zero point one degrees warmer. Bob wants us to do something about it.'

I looked over at Belle's new home. It had cost me and Jess all of our money but it was worth it to see Bob and Elle happily living together.

'I could drop in an ice-cube?' I said. 'What do you think, Mr Prickles?' I scratched him between the ears.

When we'd got back to the sanctuary that afternoon, I'd waited, pacing up and down, while the vet examined him. He really hadn't looked good and I feared the worst. It turned out that he had a broken leg, and extensive bruising to his body, but it was nothing that wouldn't heal. Every day I gave him a special exfoliating bath and rubbed him with tea tree oil, and just a few weeks later he was his awesome little self again. For a while I called him Mr Prickle-less for a joke, but his prickles had started to grow back. They were browner than they were before – he looked like a kiwi fruit.

Rex and Mrs Fernandes had allowed him to be forever-homed at my house, so he was with me all the time. In the spring I was planning to build him a cool enclosure in the garden, with a safe space for him to forage about. For now, he was content to live in my bedroom where it was warm and he could recover from his ordeal.

'I guess all we can do in life is try to treat everyone well and help them to be happy,' I said, in the manner of a wise guru, like Gandalf the wizard, or Batman's butler. 'Whether they're a new kid at school, the world's best hedgehog, or an over-fussy goldfish. If everyone did it, imagine how great the world would be.'

'That's probably the cleverest thing you've ever said.' Jess looked embarrassingly rosy and pleased. 'If you can come to that conclusion, Alex Sparrow, it gives me hope for the rest of the world.'

'Agent Alex: Bringer of Hope,' I said. 'You're not going to try to kiss me, are you, Jessticles? Because I'm really sorry to upset you but I just don't think of you that way.'

'I'm never being nice to you again.' Jess whacked me, spilling her gross hot chocolate.

'You're crushed, aren't you?'

'No, of course I'm not crushed!'

'Ah, denial. One of the many stages of crushedness,' I said. 'Don't worry, Jess. I'm sure you'll get over it in time. Maybe a year or two. Or five.'

'I'm not crushed!' She jumped off her stool in frustration.

'Ah, standing up in anger – the next stage of crushedness.'

'I hate you, sometimes, Alex!' Jess stomped out of the room.

Don't get me wrong, I actually loved Jess to bits. We'd achieved so much together, and she'd taught me more than anyone else I'd ever met. But if there was one thing I loved, it was winding her up till she was Hulk mad. I smiled and took a gulp of chocolate, cream and marshmallows.

'Mission accomplished.'

# Be a Hedgehog Hero

While lots of the aspects of Mr Prickles's character are based on fact, and the information given in reference to him is accurate, it's important to remember that he is a one-off. Hedgehogs are wild animals. They shouldn't be kept as pets and only live in forever homes when they have disabilities that mean they wouldn't survive in the wild. Hedgehogs are also vulnerable – the number of hedgehogs living in the UK is declining rapidly and we need to help them as much as we can. They are truly special animals, each with a unique appearance and colourful personality. While writing this book I was lucky enough to spend time with some gorgeous hedgehogs and hoglets, all of them in need of care – not healthy or resilient enough to survive the winter, or suffering injuries caused by gardening tools or other animals. So I'd like to ask you all to please become hedgehog heroes.

Here are some ways you can help:
Hedgehogs are nocturnal – if you see a hedgehog out and about during the day, it probably needs

help. Keep it warm and contact your nearest hedgehog rescue for advice.

Hedgehogs need to roam! You can help them by making hedgehog-sized holes in your fences so that they can move between gardens.

Providing food and a safe place to sleep can be life-saving for hedgehogs. Allow part of your garden to grow wild and build a hedgehog house with a small opening for them to come and go. Leaving shallow bowls of water and chicken-based cat or dog food outside will encourage hedgehogs to visit you. Please don't give them milk – it makes them poorly.

For more information about how you can help our hedgehogs visit www.poppyscreche.org. I'd also like to dedicate this section of the book to Ash, who inspired me to write Mr Prickles in the way that I did. I will never forget you.

# Acknowledgements

The Aviary
Helping me to fly is my amazing agent Kirsty McLachlan, to whom I owe so much, and my supportive and dedicated publishing team at Firefly Press – Janet, Rebecca, Ali, and especially Penny Thomas and Meg Farr. Thanks also to the other Firefly writers for their help and support, especially Eloise Williams.

The Incubator
Keeping me safe and warm are my Golden Egg family – Imogen Cooper, Vanessa Harbour, James Nicol, Anthony Burt, Kay Vallely, Karen Minto, Lisa Sorrell, Tristan Warner-Smith, Rus Madon, Andrew Wright, Alex Campbell, Ele Nash and Helen Clark-Jones. Special thanks to the wonderful Vashti Hardy and Lorraine Gregory – I love you lots and I simply don't know what I'd do without you. Huge thanks also to BB Taylor for her support, friendship and hedgehog help.

The Fox Run
Through triumph and defeat, I know I will have my fox pack around me – Nicola Wareing, Laura Endersby and Emma Savin. Love you always.

The Stables
Thanks to all at Waterstones Uxbridge, especially my lovely friend, Jane Carter. And to wonder-blogger Jo Clarke – your support means so much. I also want to say an enormous thank you to Ann, and to Emma and her family, at Poppy's Hedgehogs, who invited me into their homes and gave me the opportunity to witness the incredible work they do for our hedgehogs. It was a fascinating and humbling experience and I will never forget it.

Enclosure 6 – The Rabbit Paddock
My family is huge and widely spread, and have helped me so much, especially Mum, Dad, Julie and Alfie Killick. Special thanks also to all my cousins (with a big hug for Alfie Gilder) – the fact that you are proud of me means an awful lot.

The Pond

I might not see you often as we all swim around on our different journeys, but I am very grateful to lots of old friends and colleagues, especially to you, Sarah Hill and Jay Upton.

A special acknowledgement goes to the creator of Harry the horse – the brilliant and talented Sheriynta. I would also like to thank Charlotte Beck, who named Piper the rabbit; Lois Brown, who named Raymond the rat, and Charlie Sheldon, who named Sir Blimmo the tortoise.

Huge thanks to all the schools, libraries and bookshops I've visited, and the people in them who made me feel so welcome. I have met many wonderful and inspiring children on my travels and I'm thankful to every person who has read and loved Alex and Jess. A special squeeze goes to St Michael's Catholic School in High Wycombe – working with you brings me so much joy.

Enclosure 17 – Mr Prickles's Home:
I would be lost without my very own crazy and brilliant hoglets – Stanley, Teddy, Mia, Helena, Luis and Mabel. And the very prickly but incredibly gorgeous Dean Eggleton. I love you all so much.

Other books in the Alex Sparrow series:

# Alex Sparrow
# and the Really Big Stink

by Jennifer Killick

'A brilliantly bonkers, side-splitting superhero story.'
MG Leonard (*Beetle Boy*)

Alex Sparrow is a super-agent in training. He is also a human lie-detector. Working with Jess, who can communicate with animals, they must find out why their friends – and enemies – are all changing into polite and well-behaved pupils. And exactly who is behind it all.

A story of school, genius goldfish
and unexpectedly smelly superpowers.

Firefly Press, £6.99 ISBN: 9781910080566
www.fireflypress.co.uk